'I thought ... to...starting ... to each other.'

'Perhaps I misread the signs. But after you kissed me on the hill, I—'

'You mean a lot to me,' he murmured. 'An awful lot. I've never met a girl like you. But I can see what this place means to you—the country, your friends, your family. And in a year I'll be finished here. I'll be back in a hospital in some grimy bit of London. I'll be gone and you'll be here. This can only be a temporary thing and I don't want to hurt you.'

He came round to her side of the table, sat by her with his arm round her and gently kissed her. It was so good to lean against his chest, feel the warmth of his breath on her neck, the strength of his arm holding her.

'I know I shouldn't have come here,' Tom said after a while. 'I have no right to, no right at all. But I just couldn't stay away.'

'Hush,' Nikki whispered.

Gill Sanderson, aka Roger Sanderson, started writing as a husband-and-wife team. At first Gill created the storyline, characters and background, asking Roger to help with the actual writing. But her job became more and more time-consuming and he took over all of the work. He loves it!

Roger has written many Medical Romance™ books for Harlequin Mills & Boon®. Ideas come from three of his children—Helen is a midwife, Adam a health visitor, Mark a consultant oncologist. Weekdays are for work; weekends find Roger walking in the Lake District or Wales.

Recent titles by the same author:

MALE MIDWIFE
MARRIAGE AND MATERNITY
THE CONSULTANT'S RECOVERY

A DOCTOR'S COURAGE

BY
GILL SANDERSON

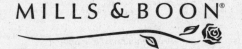

MILLS & BOON®

*All the characters in this book have no existence outside the imagination
of the author, and have no relation whatsoever to anyone bearing the
same name or names. They are not even distantly inspired by any
individual known or unknown to the author, and all the incidents are
pure invention.*

*First published in Great Britain 2002
Harlequin Mills & Boon Limited,
Eton House, 18-24 Paradise Road, Richmond, Surrey TW9 1SR*

© Gill Sanderson 2002

ISBN 0 263 83091 8

*Set in Times Roman 10½ on 12 pt.
03-0902-48173*

*Printed and bound in Spain
by Litografia Rosés, S.A., Barcelona*

CHAPTER ONE

IT WAS a fine morning in early summer when Tom dropped into Nikki Gale's life—really dropped in, that was.

It was going to be a busy day for her. But, then, all her days were busy, that was the way she liked them. Perhaps Saturday morning was different, she could take things just a bit easy. So she stayed in her dressing-gown. She listened to Radio 4, made herself a percolated cup of coffee and put on some wholemeal bread to toast. Perhaps she would sit on the little patio outside her caravan and watch the robins fly around the rather neglected back garden of the White House. How she wished she could see to that garden!

She heard it when she switched off the radio. A loud creak—and a cracking noise. It was very near, it sounded almost like a branch breaking. Her caravan was parked partly under the shade of a large oak tree. But there was no wind, not even the lightest of breezes, so why should a branch creak?

Tying her dressing-gown round her, she went outside.

Her residential caravan was parked carefully to blend in with its surroundings. It was painted dark green, situated in a grove of trees at the end of the White House garden. There was access through a high wall at the back for herself and her car.

Branches from the great oak tree hung over the

5

bedroom end of her caravan. And six feet above the van, desperately clinging onto the lowest branch, was a man.

He was facing downwards, his feet higher than his head. And just behind his feet the branch had splintered and was starting to break.

'What are you doing, climbing over my van?' Nikki asked.

The man appeared to think. 'Being over your van wasn't my precise intention,' he said after a while. 'I was trying to get to the end of this branch so I could see into that nest.'

He pointed. There was a nest where he indicated—Nikki had seen the mother robin flying to it. 'You're a bit old to be bird's-nesting,' she said severely, 'and there are no eggs there now, the chicks have hatched. It's not good to disturb them.'

'I wasn't going to disturb them,' the man said indignantly, 'I just wanted to look. I was looking out of my bedroom window and I saw a bird with a worm in its beak. It struck me that I'd never actually seen into a bird's nest with chicks. There are some things a man should do at least once in his life, and I've never seen a bird drop a worm into—'

There was no creaking this time, just a snapping sound. The branch broke and the man dropped six feet onto the caravan roof with a great thump.

'Don't try to move,' Nikki shouted. 'I'll be right up with you.' She ran to the garden shed, fetched the stepladder and propped it against the side of the van. Then she hastily climbed so she could see the van roof.

Her face was a foot away from the man's face. It was quite an attractive face. Thin perhaps, but with unusually big green eyes. His mouth looked nice but at the moment was twisted with pain or shock. And his dark hair was longish.

'I hope I haven't damaged your roof,' the man gasped politely. 'I didn't intend to fall on it.'

'It's a well-built caravan,' Nikki replied equally politely. 'I doubt whether you've harmed it much. But I'm more worried about you. Just lie there, don't try to move. Did you bang your head or hurt your neck when you fell? I'm a nurse, by the way.'

'I think I'm all right. I didn't fall too far and I managed to relax. Your roof isn't too hard either. I was winded, I'll be bruised, but most of all I'm embarrassed. Now, if you climb down I'll wriggle sideways and then come down your ladder.' He kicked the broken branch off the roof. 'I thought oak trees were supposed to be strong. This one wasn't.'

Nikki decided to defend her tree. 'It's a very thin branch,' she said, 'and you did crawl out quite a way on it. Are you sure you can climb down?'

'I think I'm fine. I just feel a fool.'

He inched towards her and she saw him wince. 'You're hurt. You look as if you might be badly bruised. When you get down I'll have a look at you.'

The man smiled. 'That'll be nice. And I can see quite a lot of you already.'

Nikki looked down and blushed. Her dressing-gown had come undone and was gaping open. As it was summer, her nightie was a bit skimpy—well, very skimpy really. He *could* see a lot of her. With one hand she managed to cover herself up. 'A gentleman wouldn't look,' she said haughtily.

'Since we were so close together, I had no choice. But you'd rather be told than not, wouldn't you?'

This is a lunatic conversation, Nikki thought.

Carefully she climbed down the ladder, steadied it and called, 'Come down now—but slowly.'

'No problem.' He slid sideways, over the edge of the van roof, his feet seeking the rungs. And two minutes later he was standing facing her. She looked at him thoughtfully.

Nikki had dealt with dozens of falls. She knew that he could be more badly injured than he realised. So many times she had seen what people had thought to be just a bruise turn out to have a broken bone underneath. And he could be suffering from shock. His face was paler than when she'd first seen him.

'Come inside and sit down,' she said. 'I'll make you a hot drink. I'm the district nurse. I'd just like to check you over a bit then we can decide if you need to go to A and E.'

'You're very kind. I don't think a visit to A and E will be necessary, but I could use a hot drink.'

She frowned. 'Do I know you? I thought I knew most people round about here.' Then she remembered something he had said and looked at him suspiciously. 'And what's this about you seeing robins from your bedroom window? What bedroom?'

The man turned and pointed to the White House. 'That bedroom. I'm living there temporarily. I'm Dr Tom Murray, I'm joining your practice. And you're Nikki Gale, the practice district nurse. Joe Kenton said that you...that you...'

Suddenly his face was even paler than before, if possible and he started to sway. 'Inside,' said Nikki, putting an arm round his waist and dragging him with her. 'You can faint there in comfort.'

But he didn't faint. She got him inside, sitting on

her banquette, opened a window next to him and made him a cup of the traditional sweet tea. A couple of minutes later she saw the colour creeping back into his cheeks. 'Don't try to talk,' she said, 'just sit there.'

He did try to object a bit later when she told him she was going to take his pulse and blood pressure. But then she said, 'You're a doctor. What would you do if I had fallen?'

'You're a persuasive woman, District Nurse Gale. I suppose you're right.'

Both pulse and BP were within acceptable limits—though she thought just a bit high. Then she told him to take off his shirt and let her see his arm, chest and shoulder—the bits she knew he had fallen on.

He was going to be bruised and there was a nasty gash on his ribs where he had caught himself on the corner of one of her skylights. She bathed the cut, pulled it together with butterfly stitches. Then she felt his arms and shoulders, got him to stand and move everything. She could tell it hurt, but there didn't seem to be any bones broken. 'No serious damage,' she said, 'though you should take painkillers if it hurts too much.'

'I'll do that.' He shrugged back into his shirt and she sat to watch him. He had a lean body, sinewy, no fat on him at all. It was almost as if he'd decided to slim far beyond what was necessary. Like a jockey, in fact, but he was too tall and well built to be a jockey.

'You're a good patient,' she said when he had his shirt back on. 'Most doctors aren't.'

'I've learned always to do what nurses—and doctors—tell me. Makes for a quiet life. And now we've

finished the medical bit, we can be formally introduced.' He held out his hand. 'I'm Dr Tom Murray,
and, as I said, we're going to be neighbours and
we're going to work together. I'm pleased to meet
you, Nikki. I can tell you're a real asset to the practice.'

She took his hand, feeling ridiculously pleased,
and looked at him for the first time as a man, not as
a trespasser or a patient.

He was casually dressed—old trainers without
socks, khaki drill trousers, a disreputable shirt with
the collar torn off, now stained with blood, and li-
chen from the branch. She had noticed the long hair
before, it gave a more cheerful effect to what could
have been a severe face. It was a thin face—with
lines around the eyes as if he frowned a lot. But there
was that generous mouth and those gorgeous green
eyes…

With a start she realised that she was still holding
his hand. Quickly letting it go, she said, 'Since we're
going to be neighbours, would you like to stay for
breakfast?'

'I'd be delighted. But…' He indicated her dressing-gown and slippers. 'Haven't I caught you un-
awares?'

'Oh. Well, yes. Why don't you go and sit on my
patio if you feel up to it? It'll only take me a minute
to get dressed. Here, take the paper and read while
you wait.'

Nikki slipped into her tiny bathroom for a quick
wash, then went to her equally tiny bedroom. After
vigorously brushing her hair, she found herself looking at a long dress. She knew she looked well in it
and… Not on a warm Saturday morning! She put on

shorts and a T-shirt. But she did add a touch of lipstick. It wasn't often that she had a guest for breakfast!

In the kitchen she put on coffee to percolate and made more toast. Then she placed things on a tray and took it out to where Tom was sitting, waiting for her. He stood as she came down the steps and took the tray from her. She liked that.

She poured the coffee and passed him the toast. It was very pleasant, sitting out here on her patio in early summer, with…well, say it, a good-looking man with her. It wasn't usual.

'I knew you were coming,' she said, 'but I was away on a course when you came up for interview and to look round. Why the big change? I gather you were a junior registrar in a big London hospital—specialising in orthopaedics wasn't it? There was a distinguished career in front of you.'

'Possibly distinguished.' He smiled. 'But perhaps just ordinary.'

'So why change? Why come to be a rural practice GP in the Yorkshire moors?'

'Well, I did train to be a GP first, in London. Then I got interested in orthopaedics, was offered a good job and…' He shrugged. 'But then I changed my mind.' He waved his hand around to point at the trees, the birds, the sky. 'Look at all this. I've lived all my life in London. Nothing but work as far back as I can remember—you know, the usual fourteen-hour day. One day it struck me, I loved the countryside and yet I'd not been out of town for over nine months. So I gave up the job—for a year. For a year I'll do something completely different. I know I'll have to work here, and I want to. But I'm thirty-one.

There's so many things I haven't done yet, and I'm going to do some of them.'

'Like fall onto a caravan roof?'

'Exactly. I had it on my list of things I must do, now I can happily cross it off.'

Nikki was enjoying herself. She liked this new colleague. 'My mother says I'm nosy,' she said, 'I prefer to say that I'm naturally curious. How come you're living in the White House? I should tell you, I envy you. I've wanted to live there since I was a little girl.'

He laughed. 'You know I'm doing a year's locum work because Anna Rix is taking maternity leave?'

'Yes. She's married to an American, Floyd Rix. They've gone back to America for a while.'

'Well, she wanted the house to be used and so I'm leasing it for a year. It couldn't have worked out better. Joe Kenton suggested it. You've been inside, haven't you?'

'Of course. Lots of times. And each time I find myself thinking that I'd have things a bit different from Anna. But it's a wonderful house.'

'It is. It's the largest place I've ever lived in. I've tended to have just a tiny central flat and use it for nothing much but sleeping. Now I'm looking forward to learning to cook and perhaps even learning to garden. So, tell me how you come to be my neighbour.'

Nikki shrugged. 'The house used to belong to Joe. He offered me this place to live when I came to be his practice nurse six years ago. We both thought it would be a temporary thing—but I never got round to moving. Then when Anna bought the house she was happy for me to stay—I help her with the garden sometimes. I like the place.' She looked at Tom's empty plate and mug. 'More toast and coffee?'

'Please. I'm really enjoying this, Nikki. You must come over and have a meal with me when I get my-self properly settled.'

'I'd like that. Er, will you be…that is…'

He grinned. 'You're trying to find a tactful way of asking if I'm married. No, you won't have a new lady neighbour. And there's no fiancée or other woman waiting for me in the background. It's a dreadful thing to say, but I've been so busy working that the relationships I've had tended to be…well, over fairly quickly. Now, since it's let's-be-frank time, tell me about yourself. A good-looking woman like you must have a man somewhere—if not two or three.'

She liked being told she was good-looking and smiled. 'At the moment, I don't have a man in my life. Perhaps I'm too busy as well.'

Then she hastily gathered crockery onto the tray and ran inside. Maybe things were moving just a touch too fast for her.

Tom didn't hear Nikki coming back when she came back to the door with her freshly laden tray. She saw him staring across the White House lawn with an expression of…it looked like sadness on his face. It was too fine a day to be sad.

She put her tray on the table and said, 'You looked a bit pensive then. Not pining for the bright lights of London, were you?'

Tom laughed. 'No. Just a twinge from where I fell, I guess. In a minute I'll go to have a bath and see if that helps to soothe things.'

'Good idea,' she said. Privately, she thought that

what she'd seen hadn't looked like physical pain. Still, who could tell? She passed him his coffee and the plate of toast.

'I like to see a girl with an appetite,' he said, 'but how come you can eat such a hearty breakfast and still remain thin?'

'The word I prefer is slim,' she told him. 'Thin is bad but slim is good. And don't forget you're working out in the moors now. There'll be a lot of climbing to out-of-the-way cottages and farms in distant places. Anyway, you can't talk. You're all muscle and bone. How come you're so slim—or thin?'

'A lot of exercise in the gym,' he said after a pause. 'One thing I am looking forward to is walking a bit more. In fact, walking a lot more.'

'Around here is good for walking. In fact, there's—' Her mobile phone rang. 'Excuse me a minute.' She went back inside the caravan to pick up the phone.

It was Joe Kenton, the senior partner of the practice. 'I'm having breakfast with Tom, your new recruit,' she told Joe. 'He seems a nice fellow.'

'He is indeed,' said Joe after a pause. 'Of course, living next door, you'll see quite a lot of him. We were very lucky to get someone for a year. But, then, in time he'll be off… Nikki, I know you're not on call but have you anything on this morning?'

'Nothing I can't put on hold. Why, are there problems?'

'Well, I've got some people coming round to see me who I can't really put off. And I've just had a phone call from the Abbott's Farm Campsite. A mother there wants me to leave out a prescription for her child. He's got a sudden fever. I'm just a little worried… If you're anywhere, near could you call?'

She knew the campsite he referred to, a good one. 'I'll call round,' she said. 'It's probably nothing but it's a good idea to make sure.' Something struck her. 'As I've got Tom here,' she said, 'if he's got nothing else to do, he might like to have a wander round, get to know the area. It's a glorious day for going out.'

'Good idea,' Joe said heavily. 'Let him see what country work is like. Now, phone me if there's any great problem.' He rang off.

She went back outside. 'I've got to put my uniform on,' she said to Tom. 'We've got a case up on the moors.' She told him what Joe had told her. Then, a bit too casually, she said, 'I know you said you were going to have a bath, and you really ought to rest, but if you wanted to have a look round and see a bit of the area, you could come with me. Of course, you might have something else to do.'

'I'd love to come with you,' he said with a smile. 'I can get to know the area and get to know you, too. I think the relationship between a doctor and a nurse is very important. We'll be working together so we need to get to know each other.'

'Of course,' she said. It made sense. But why did she feel so ridiculously pleased?

Tom went to get changed, Nikki went to put on her uniform. Just before she pulled the blue dress over her head she looked at herself in the mirror. Thin or slim? Slim, she decided. Thin people didn't have the firm breasts that she had or the definite curve between waist and hips. She decided he'd called her thin because of her long legs. She knew they were one of her best features. She had to face it, her legs were one of the reasons she'd put on shorts when she'd changed out of her dressing-gown.

And her face was…well, it was all right. She had short, thick blonde hair in a bob. And, yes, she'd had compliments about her face. Quite a few, in fact.

Feeling just a touch embarrassed at this self-inventory, she dragged the uniform over her head. Why were her looks suddenly so important?

When Tom came back fifteen minutes later he had changed into something more formal and was carrying a doctor's bag. 'I know you'll have your own bag,' he said, 'but I'll bring mine just in case. Never know what might be needed.'

'True,' she said. 'Let's get going.'

He looked doubtfully at her rather battered four-wheel-drive car, and then climbed up into the passenger's seat. 'Not the car I usually expect a district nurse to have,' he said. 'I was thinking of something small and placid.'

Nikki laughed. 'It's summer now. But when winter comes, the hills around here can have a foot or more of snow—and then it drifts. That's when you need the height and the traction. What kind of car have you got?'

He laughed in his turn. 'At the moment, a low, fast sports car. But I guess I'll have to change it when we get nearer winter. Shall we go?'

Tom was silent for a while as she drove quickly through Hambleton and out onto the moors. Then he said, 'I can see you look around, smell the air, look contented. You're happy here, aren't you?'

She wondered at this observation, and was rather pleased at it. 'This is where I was born, this is where

I belong. I love it here, I could never leave this area. I hope you'll be happy here, too.'

'Well, I certainly intend to do all the things I've never done in my urban life. I've got a lot to cram in in a short time.'

She was surprised at the note of determination in his voice.

Seven miles out of Hambleton she swung into the entrance to Abbott's Farm Campsite. 'We see a lot of holidaymakers in the surgery,' she told Tom. 'People come here for the walking and…' she shuddered '…for the caving. So we get a lot of problems not usually seen in winter. A fair number of gastric upsets. The odd bad cut or bruise or broken bone when someone's been scrambling among the rocks—kids are the worst for that. And, of course, the ever-present sunburn.'

They pulled up outside the camp shop, looked at the neat piles of food and supplies, the locked-up gas cylinders some distance away. 'We'll check in with Maureen Abbott. She knows everything that happens on this site.'

'The Jenny Hudson family,' Maureen said, looking with some interest at Tom. 'They're a nice lot. I hope the little boy's all right. They're down at the bottom field, four big tents with a central kitchen. Only the women and children left, the men drove off early this morning. They've gone caving.'

Nikki looked amazed. 'A glorious day like this and they've gone crawling through a nasty wet dark hole in the ground.'

'I know,' said Maureen, 'but we get a lot who come here just for that. Let me know if there's anything I can do for the little lad.'

As they drove down to the bottom field, Nikki said to Tom, 'We have to decide on something. Are you making this visit or am I?'

'I don't officially start until Monday so I'd prefer you to deal with this. But if you like, I'll hover round and help if necessary.'

'That's fine.' She thought he'd said the right thing—Joe had asked her to deal with this, not him.

She was impressed by the camp. As Maureen had said, there were four large tents round a central shelter for cooking and dining. Everything was neat and tidy—by no means the usual case.

As they stopped, a woman came out of one of the tents. She was fair and wore shorts, and had a worried expression on her face. 'Hi, I'm Nikki Gale, District Nurse,' Nikki said. 'This is Dr Tom Murray, a colleague. I gather you have a sick child here?'

'Oh, I'm so glad you've come,' the woman burst out. 'I'm Jenny Hudson. It's my son, Eric. I think he's getting worse, I was even thinking about calling the ambulance. It's probably just a holiday thing, but none of the other kids have got it and I do feel a bit lonely here away from my own kitchen.'

'You're on your own?'

'No. The other mums have taken the kids to the playground so Eric isn't disturbed. I can shout them if they're needed. And our husbands are down Lassen's Pot. They set off before we were awake.'

'Rather them than me,' said Nikki, with feeling. 'Now, let's have a look at this little lad.'

He was lying in one of the tents, lethargic, with a high temperature. He had refused anything to eat. 'I wondered,' said Jenny, 'since he's done and eaten exactly the same as all the rest of the kids…I wondered if it was…it was…'

Nikki had scanned the little body for a rash, tested the neck for stiffness. 'It's not meningitis,' she said. 'That's definite. You thought that, didn't you?'

Jenny looked confused. 'Well, you hear so many stories…'

'Don't worry, you were right to call us. Did he spend a lot of time out in the sun yesterday?'

The woman looked doubtful. 'Well, yes. But all the rest of the kids did, too.'

'He's very fair, like you. I'd say he's suffering from mild sunstroke. It affects some people but not others. Now, keep him inside. Give him fluids—as much as he will take. Don't worry about feeding him, he'll eat when he's ready. And when he does finally go out, slather him in a barrier cream and make him wear a hat.'

Nikki glanced at Tom who nodded in agreement.

Jenny looked relieved. 'Only sunstroke? You must think me a hysterical mother, dragging you out like this for something so unimportant.'

'We don't think you're hysterical,' said Nikki, 'and don't ever think that sunstroke is unimportant.'

She bent, stroked the child's cheek and pulled up the sheet round him. 'Just let him sleep for a while now. And if he gets worse, by all means phone us again.'

There were the inevitable forms to fill in, and Jenny poured them some iced lemonade as they sat under the kitchen awning.

'My husband's down in his cave,' she said. 'He'll be really enjoying himself, they've been planning this trip for a year. He'd never have gone if he'd known Eric was sick—he's our first child.'

Nikki shivered. 'Caving? Why do it? I can see the point of rock-climbing—in fact, I've done a bit. But slithering around in the dark and wet, with the thought of all that rock pressing down on top of you? It's madness!'

Jenny smiled and shook her head. 'It's just got something,' she said. 'Why not try it some time?'

'I'd like to try,' Tom said thoughtfully. 'It would be a brand-new experience.'

Nikki shook her head. 'I'd be terrified. Closed spaces—they make me feel claustrophobic.'

Tom laughed. 'You'd be lost in London. I travel everywhere by tube.'

'The few occasions I go to London, I always travel by bus.'

She didn't like to say so but it was more than terror on her part. All her life she'd been unable to go into confined spaces. She just couldn't do it.

Tom was quiet again on their way back. He stared out of the window, occasionally asking her the name of a hill or a village. He seemed to take great interest in all that was around him—she supposed it was a complete contrast with his life in London.

Nikki liked his company, she decided, and would like to spend more time with him. But she mustn't be too pushy. At least, being neighbours would be a good start. They could take things easily and see how it went from there.

'I'll drop these papers into the surgery and have a quick word with Joe,' Nikki said when they reached Hambleton again. 'Do you want to come with me?'

'I think I'll have that bath and do a little unpacking,' he said. 'This quiet country life is going to take some getting used to—it's harder than London.'

She giggled. 'You'll get used to it in time. I'll drop you off at the White House.'

'So what will you do for the rest of the day?' Tom asked.

She didn't need asking twice. 'Tonight I'm stage manager for the Hambleton Players. I've been assistant stage manager for the last two nights—that means power without responsibility—but tonight I'm it. The regular manager has got to go to a wedding or something.'

'I like going to plays,' he said, sounding genuinely interested. 'Tell me more.'

'Well, it's a thriller called *Death at Night*. It'll be a sell-out again, it always is. There'll even be a few who haven't paid standing at the back. Thursday night and last night went well, but tonight's the night. If we do well tonight, we'll be the talk of the town for weeks to come.' She glanced at him sideways. 'In fact, I could do with a gofer. There'll be a couple of people missing tonight.'

'A gofer?'

'Goes for things. Make tea, fetch and carry, look for props, see to the curtains, call people when they're on, be a runner for the electrician.'

'Sounds like my kind of job. Do you want a volunteer?'

Definitely she wanted a volunteer. Especially Tom. But she said coolly, 'All right, then, if you like. It's in the Assembly Rooms, the hall right next to the church. You can't miss it. Be there by six this evening and wear old clothes.'

'I'm looking forward to it.'

Shortly afterwards she dropped him off at the White House. Then she drove off to see Joe.

The Moors Surgery was an old Victorian building which had been expertly added to and altered to make it efficient as well as handsome. Nikki drove into the large car park, locked her car and went inside. She picked up her mail and checked her lists for the next Tuesday and Thursday afternoons—which was when she ran her well-woman clinics. Then she filed the report on Eric Hudson and sat in the tearoom to wait for a word with Joe.

Eventually he came out of his meeting. A tall, straight-backed sixty-year-old, with a manner that sometimes betrayed his eight years in the army.

'The man who manages to separate paperwork from medicine will earn my undying gratitude,' he said, stretching out his fingers. 'I think I've got writer's cramp.'

'You always say that patients' notes must be kept up to date—and I agree.' She smiled.

'Well, patients' notes are different. How was your trip onto the moors?'

She told him about Eric. Then she went on, 'I think I'm going to like working with Tom Murray. He seems a good doctor.'

'Yes,' Joe said heavily, 'we're very lucky to get him. But he's only here for a year. Don't get too attached to...working with him. In a year's time he'll be out of your life for good.'

Nikki laughed. 'He's a colleague, that's all.'

'Of course he is. But after a year he'll go. And you'll stay here in the Yorkshire moors. You couldn't move anywhere else, could you?'

'No. This is my home, and this is where I'm going to stay.'

As she drove home she wondered why Joe—a true friend, she knew—had chosen to warn her against any kind of involvement with Tom in that oblique fashion.

CHAPTER TWO

THE Thursday and Friday night performances of the play had been well received, but Saturday night was the all-important night. The hall would be crammed full, so they had to do well. This would be a topic of conversation for weeks to come.

Nikki was a bit nervous—there was a lot for the stage manager to do and this wasn't her usual kind of work. But she would manage.

She was at the Assembly Rooms early. Much to her surprise, Tom came shortly afterwards. He was escorted backstage by Anthea Brown, a very attractive local girl who had a walk-on part. Anthea had her arm firmly through Tom's.

'Tom here says he's come to help you,' Anthea said, and winked at Nikki from behind Tom's back.

'Good to see you, Tom,' said Nikki. 'Thanks for showing him the way, Anthea.'

It took Anthea a minute to realise that she was being dismissed. She grinned, winked at Nikki again and said, 'I'll be looking forward to seeing you at the party afterwards, Tom.' Then she was gone.

'Party?' asked Tom. 'I didn't know there was a party. I haven't got my party frock on.'

'Just a way of relaxing,' Nikki said, 'nothing too serious. We'll need it after the past three days.'

It was only a few hours since she'd seen Tom, only a few hours since she'd met him for the first time, and she was slightly shocked at how pleased she felt to be with him again.

He was dressed in a black T-shirt and jeans, and the starkness of the outfit emphasised the wiriness of his body, the almost gaunt lines of his face. Of course, when he smiled it was different, and she smiled back happily.

'I'm here to work,' he said. 'And, please, no talk of medicine. I want to lift and fetch and carry.'

'You're going to be more than useful,' said Nikki. 'Incidentally, how's the side? Are you up to this? No pain, no stiffness?'

'We doctors are accustomed to pain—usually other people's, though. No, I'm fine.'

'In that case, come to the front of house.' She showed him the stacks of chairs ranged round the side of the hall. 'These should all be in rows. Will you start by arranging them? The marks are here on the floor.'

'No problem.' He nodded cheerfully. 'You're not going to help me?'

'No. I'm going to check what I've got to do backstage. Don't be afraid if you hear all sorts of odd sounds.'

She scurried back to work. There was a short tape of a car crash, a pistol to be fired three times, sundry knocks on a door, a scream off and the sheet to be shaken that gave a very believable rendition of thunder. Nikki worked her way through them all, then put everything necessary carefully on her backstage table. There also was her tattered script and a big notice saying, DON'T EVEN THINK ABOUT TOUCHING ANY OF THESE. All was in order.

She went back to see how Tom was getting on.

Very well! He was being helped in his task by
Anthea and her friend. So far nothing had made these
two work. Nikki wondered how he had done it—then
guessed that she knew.

As she looked she saw Tom wince and put his
hand to his back. 'You OK, Tom?' she called in concern.

'Just a twinge—perhaps a bit of bruising from that
fall,' he called back carelessly. 'Nothing to worry
about.'

'Well, when you've finished, could you come
backstage and help me check the lighting plot?'

'Can you help me with this pile of chairs first,
Tom?' Anthea said, obviously not intending to be left
out. Nikki grinned and left them to it.

He was with her ten minutes later. 'We have to
check the lighting plot,' she told him. 'We've got a
volunteer electrician—Gordon Glaze of Gordon's
Electrical Supplies down the high street. He loves his
work and he's good at it. Unfortunately, he thinks
that people come to see the lighting effects, not the
play. I've never seen an amateur production with
such a good lightning storm.'

Tom laughed. 'I've met anaesthetists like that,' he
said.

The play went brilliantly. Nikki stayed at her desk,
sending Tom to do whatever she needed. He did it
all happily. At the end there was lots of applause and
she and the director had to appear on stage. He had
changed into a dinner jacket, she had to appear in
scruffy jeans and shirt. It had all gone very well, but
finally the audience filed out and the party could
begin.

Still acting as her gofer, Tom appeared with a plastic cup of white wine and a paper plate of salad and pork pie for her. She realised she was famished. 'It's a new and different life backstage, isn't it?' she asked him.

'Different from medicine, but not all that new—three weeks ago I was backstage in the National Theatre.'

'The National! How did you get there?'

'There's an actress there who's a very good friend of mine. I treated her once and now we go to a lot of places together.'

Perhaps her face hinted at what she was thinking, because he went on, 'She's very good at playing older women—she's sixty-three.'

Nikki felt better, and then felt angry at herself. What did it matter to her how old Tom's female friends were?

It was a good party. There was more to be eaten and more lukewarm white wine to be drunk. Nikki introduced Tom to the various people as the new doctor. He became instantly popular—especially among the women.

Someone persuaded Gordon to put dance music on his PA system and Anthea came over in a new dress, her lipstick freshly applied. 'Going to dance with me, Tom?' she asked. 'Somebody's got to get people started.'

Tom shook his head. 'Thanks, Anthea, but, no, I'm too old for this kind of music. Why don't you ask that lad over there? He looks as if he can move.'

Anthea turned to survey the lad indicated. 'Jerry Harris? Well, I suppose he'll do, but I'd rather dance with you.'

'I hurt my back this morning, I need to rest it. Now, off you go.'

Realising she would get nowhere, Anthea sighed and drifted away.

'You've made a conquest,' Nikki whispered.

'She'll be a very attractive girl in a year or two. But at the moment a little young for me. And far too energetic.'

He indicated the floor, where Anthea and Jerry were dancing.

Soon the party was over. 'If you like, you could go over to the Tinsley Arms with the rest of them,' Nikki suggested to Tom. 'They'll be having a few more drinks there.'

'What are you doing?'

'Well, a small group stays behind to wash and clear up. It's always the backstage staff's job.'

'That's what I am so that's what I'll do.'

The next time she saw him he was standing at a sink full of suds with an apron round his waist. 'Different from backstage at the National Theatre,' Nikki teased.

'Very different. But much more fun.' She felt warm when he said that.

When all was finished she asked Tom again if he wanted to go to the Tinsley Arms. But she noticed he was looking tired, and she wasn't surprised when he said no. They walked home together through the silent streets of Hambleton, she chatting idly about her work as a district nurse, he explaining what was so interesting in orthopaedics. Nikki was pleased to talk about neutral matters. She needed a rest.

They seemed to have come a long way since he'd fallen into her life that morning. He walked her down the lane at the back of the White House. She unlocked the door in the high wall and moved to where her porch light had been left on.

'It's been interesting meeting you, Tom Murray,' she said.

It had been a good day, but she was tired and had drunk a couple of glasses of wine. She liked this man and thought he liked her. So she leaned forward to kiss him on the cheek. Just a friendly kiss, nothing more. Then he put his hand on her waist and kissed her back—on the cheek. But somehow the moment lasted longer than they had both intended. Then he released her. It had just been a friendly kiss. Hadn't it?

'Goodnight, Tom,' she whispered, hoping he couldn't detect the tremor in her voice. 'I think this is a good time for me to go to bed.'

'Goodnight, Nikki.' He waited till she had let herself into her caravan, then walked swiftly to the back of the White House.

She showered, got ready for bed then peered out of her window. Dimly she could see the lights on in the White House. She wondered what Tom was doing. Which bedroom was his? Was he...? She shrugged and reached for a magazine. Better not to be silly. They had only just met.

For two days they didn't see each other again. The Sunday Nikki spent with her parents at their farm. On Monday she called in at the surgery before setting off on her rounds. Tom was there, apparently having a long talk with Joe, so she didn't disturb them. On Monday evening she visited friends in town. She had a very busy social life and she wondered how Tom was managing in a town where he knew virtually no one—no one but her, that was.

It was late Tuesday afternoon before she saw him again. She had just had an enjoyable but tiring session with her well-woman clinic. She expected to get more work now. Some of their female patients preferred to discuss their intimate problems with another woman, and since Anna Rix had left Nikki had been the only woman available. The last three clients had wanted advice on hormone replacement therapy, and this was something that Nikki had specialised in.

Her last patient had gone and she was about to relax with a well-earned drink. She wondered if she'd see Tom, then she could ask him how his first couple of days had gone.

Their meeting wasn't as she'd anticipated. Tom put his head round the door and said, 'We've got an emergency coming in. Would you like to come and help?' His voice was cold, angry even.

'Of course. What kind of emergency?'

It was more than a few miles to the nearest A and E department. Quite often emergencies came into the surgery which in a town would have been sent straight to hospital.

'A suicide—or attempted suicide. An overdose. A twenty-one-year-old girl, apparently dumped by her boyfriend. This is her way of getting even. Her name is Leni Simmonds.' His voice still sounded angry.

'I know the family—in fact, I've treated Leni. She tends to be a bit hysterical. She had a lot of time off school because she just couldn't get on. What did she take an overdose of?' This was all-important to know.

'Aspirin, I think. I talked to her father, he says she

only took one of those small packets—I think they hold sixteen.'

Nikki nodded, then, taking in Tom's stormy face, was driven to ask if he was OK.

'I don't like suicides,' Tom growled.

Silently, Nikki agreed. This was a common complaint of doctors and nurses. But, then, she and Tom were professionals, they should take these things in their stride.

They heard a car draw up outside, and went to lead the weeping Leni and her mother and father into the surgery. Nikki took Leni through into the treatment room while Tom stayed to ask the parents a few questions. Then, together, they examined Leni.

Her father had already made her vomit but Tom decided to give her gastric lavage anyway. It was a messy business, more commonly done in a hospital than a GP's surgery, but Tom thought it worthwhile. Then they decided that Leni could go home. Nikki said she would call, but that Leni would have to be referred for psychiatric counselling. There was no point in talking to her now.

Afterwards Nikki and Tom sat together in the doctors' lounge. 'This isn't orthopaedics, is it?' she challenged.

'No. But I've done my time in general medicine, and more than a little in A and E. I know what it's like. And I hate suicides and attempted suicides even more!'

She was surprised at his vehemence. 'I understand,' she said, 'but can't you see they are cries for help? Can't you show them some sympathy?'

'That girl showed sympathy for no one! How would her parents have felt if she'd succeeded?

They're good people, I liked them. And their daughter could have woken up, decided to change her mind and twenty-four hours later she's dead. I've seen it happen!'

'You seem to feel very strongly about it,' Nikki said gently. 'Have you...did you lose someone you loved that way?'

She could see he was trying to calm himself, trying to be once more the urbane man of before.

'No, I haven't lost any one I loved,' he said. 'It's just cases I've come across. Life is a gift that shouldn't be thrown away. It's the most precious gift we have, Nikki! Perhaps only when you're in danger of losing it do you value it most. So maybe Leni will learn something from this.'

'I've not seen much of you,' she said, 'but I don't believe that you're an angry man. I think most of the time you're calm. Why are you angry now?'

'I'd rather be calm. Sorry, Nikki, this is just my hobby-horse. Let's forget it, I'm all right now.'

But she thought that in his past there was some reason for his anger. Perhaps one day he would tell her.

Nikki went back to her van, cooked herself a light meal and enjoyed it out on her patio. An ordinary, pleasant evening, a change from the occasional trials of the day. Then she thought about the coming evening.

She didn't like to think of herself as forward, and the very thought of throwing herself at a man made her feel ill. But she wanted to be hospitable. What would she want if she were Tom and had just come to this village?

She thought about it and at half past eight she phoned him on his mobile phone.

'Hi, Tom,' she said, hoping her voice sounded suitably nonchalant, not excited or hopeful. 'I just wondered if you fancied a walk down to the Tinsley Arms. There's an outreach class in first aid in the Assembly Rooms that finishes at nine o'clock on Tuesdays. A pal of mine runs it, and afterwards a few friends gather for a quick drink afterwards. Would you like to come? Or you could drop in later if you're busy.' Tom's pause made her feel flustered, so she blurted out, 'This isn't a date or anything— just a chance to meet a few of the local people.'

His voice sounded amused. 'I'm not going to come if it isn't a date. I'd love to come and I wouldn't dream of dropping in later. Shall I call for you in fifteen minutes?'

'Fine,' she said. When they'd rung off she desperately wondered what she should wear.

Usually she wore jeans—or shorts in this hot weather. No one else would be smartly dressed, but she decided that there was a line between casual and scruffy. She didn't want to cross it.

Eventually she found a light blue dress that was summery and went well with her blonde hair and tan. It's just because I want to feel good in myself, she thought, I'm not trying to impress anyone. But she still turned out the bottom of her wardrobe, searching for a pair of her favorite white sandals.

He looked well, too. He seemed to like black, but this time he wasn't wearing a T-shirt but one in some kind of expensive cotton, the sleeves rolled loosely to his forearms. She felt a little thrill when she saw him.

'Just thought you might like to meet a few more people socially,' she told him. 'This is quite a tight community.'

He nodded gravely. 'It'll be good to see people not from the wrong side of a doctor's desk,' he said.

'Exactly.' She smiled.

They strolled down through Hambleton. She loved this town. As ever, she nodded, said hello to all kinds of people. This was a community and she was a part of it. Perhaps, in time, Tom would be a part of it, too. When they arrived at the Tinsley Arms she led the way to the back room.

There were a couple of dozen people there, roughly all the same age. She had been to school with more than a few of them. She peered through the glass door, and frowned as she noticed one particular man. She put up a hand to stop Tom opening the door.

'Just before we go in,' she said, 'see the man at the bar in the brown jacket?'

'The one throwing peanuts up and trying to catch them in his mouth? Seems happy enough,' said Tom.

'He is—or he was. His name's Toby Lowe, I've known him all my life. About a year ago he had a terrible motorbike accident and fractured his skull. He wasn't expected to live but he did. Trouble is, since then he's suffered from a form of epilepsy— he doesn't have fits but has really violent mood swings. He can't hold a job down, he gets depressed and then he won't take his medication. So he gets worse still. His mother's called me a couple of times and usually I've been to talk him into it. But once he starts drinking…there's trouble.'

'I think that pint glass is full of orange juice,' murmured Tom. 'He should be all right.'

They went inside, where he bought her a white wine and had a bitter himself. Then she introduced him to the group. He fitted in at once.

'Hey, Nikki,' Toby called, 'look who's being a good boy.' He held his glass up. 'Orange juice only. I'm celebrating, I've been offered a job on Hanley's Farm.'

'Oh, Toby, that's great! When you finish that one I'll buy you another to celebrate.'

'I'll move onto grapefruit,' Toby threatened.

She was pleased for him. The contrast between the shy boy he had been and the unpleasant creature he could turn into now was always painful. Perhaps a regular job would sort him out.

Nikki started off talking with Tom at her side, but things didn't work that way in the group. She was called to one side and asked for a bit of personal advice on contraception by a worried friend. Then she was invited to admire a new pendant, a fifth wedding anniversary present. In his turn Tom found himself drawn into a detailed discussion on sports car engines.

But after an hour they were in the same small group when a voice at her elbow said, 'Won't you introduce me to your new friend, Nikki?' Nikki thought the voice unnecessarily husky.

'Of course,' she said, trying to disguise vague feelings of irritation. 'Meriel, this is Tom Murray, he's our new doctor. Tom, this is Meriel McCarthy. She's… What are you doing now Meriel?'

Meriel didn't answer. In a room full of people dressed casually, she stood out. Her hair and make-up were perfect. She wore an obviously expensive dress with layers of floating white chiffon. Meriel stood out. She always did.

'It's so good to meet someone new,' she murmured to Tom. 'Did I hear that you were from London?'

'Just here for a year,' said Tom. 'I'm very much looking forward to working in Hambleton. May I get you a drink?'

After that Meriel seemed to be in every group that Tom was with. Nikki didn't really mind. Meriel was the town vamp, everyone knew that. She was the daughter of the richest farmer of the area and was very discontented with life in Hambleton. Nikki hoped that Tom was shrewd enough to see through her.

The group always broke up early as it was a weekday. Nikki thought that Tom looked a bit tired—he'd had a busy last few days after all. 'No hurry, but I'm ready to go when you are,' she whispered to him.

'Right now would suit me. Do we just shout a general goodbye or—?'

From somewhere Meriel appeared. 'Not leaving?' she asked Tom. 'I was going to ask you back to the house for a coffee. And you, of course, Nikki.'

'Thank you but no,' Tom said firmly. 'Perhaps another time.'

'I'll hold you to that.' Meriel touched Tom's arm with one elegantly manicured hand. 'It's been so nice to meet you, Tom.'

And after that, Tom and Nikki were allowed to leave.

They walked back through the town. 'I liked the atmosphere there,' Tom said. 'It was casual and relaxed. Most of you have known each other for years. It's all new to me. Any gatherings like this I've been to in London are often a bit…competitive. Highly charged, in fact.'

They walked on a bit in companionable silence and then he said, with humour in his voice, 'Meriel's a nice girl, isn't she?'

'Very nice,' said Nikki. She felt reassured, sure that Tom was more interested in her than Meriel. She felt even more reassured when he took her hand.

It had only been three days since she'd met Tom for the first time. But they got on well and she wondered if what had started as simple friendship might turn into something more. Once again he walked her to her front door, and this time he kissed her on the lips. At first it was a gentle, a tentative kiss but then it turned into something else. He put his arms round her, pulling her to him, and she hugged him back, holding all of her against him. She felt vaguely alarmed, she hadn't known that she could feel so strongly about someone she had known such a short time. But the feeling was there. And she knew he shared it. For a while it was sheer bliss. But then, to her disappointment, he eased her away.

'I've just got here, Nikki,' he said gently. 'We hardly know each other, we have to work together and we have to remember that in a year's time I'll be gone. I like you…I like you a lot. I just don't want to feel I'm leading you on. I don't want to hurt you.'

'I'm a big girl, I can look after myself. You won't hurt me, I know that. So kiss me again and then you can go.'

He did kiss her again. Again it was a gentle kiss

at first, but soon she could feel the passion stirring in both of them. She could have stayed there for ever. But then he released her, muttered goodnight and turned to walk to the White House.

A good evening, she thought as she got ready for bed, a good, good evening. She was getting to know Tom. She liked him such a lot—not that liking was the right word. She suspected she was to feel something much deeper. It was sweet that he didn't want to hurt her. But she was sure that he wouldn't.

CHAPTER THREE

ON FRIDAY morning Nikki took Tom with her on another call out on the moors. There was a couple she had been visiting regularly and she'd suggested to Joe that perhaps it was time that a doctor saw them. Joe had agreed, and had told her to ask Tom.

It was a pleasant drive. They swooped down side roads, looking at the grey rocks pushing through the greenness of the summer grass. Tom again said little. He appeared to enjoy the scenery as much as she did, staring at the ghylls and sheep-scattered fields. She was content not to talk, happy just to be with him.

Eventually her four-wheel-drive turned off a side road and bumped down a steep track to a little stone farmhouse at the bottom of the valley.

'George and Mary Dunmore used to farm this land,' Nikki explained. 'It's not very productive and it was a hard life. Now they still live in the farm-house but they lease out the land and buildings to a neighbouring farmer. I visit regularly and do what I can, but I think things are getting worse.'

'What are the problems exactly?'

'Basically they're both getting old. They have no family—Mary couldn't have children. George's rheumatoid arthritis is now so bad that he's virtually bedridden and Mary has to do everything for him. She has difficulty coping and got so upset about it that Joe had to prescribe a sedative for her—she's on diazepam. And we can't organise too much help for

her out here—there's no way we could get a home
help to come this far.'

Nikki pointed over her shoulder at a set of carriers
on the back seat. 'I phone her every time I'm going
to come out and ask what she wants from the shops.
About once a week I call in with her groceries.'

'Not usually part of a district nurse's job,' Tom
said thoughtfully.

'It helps them no end. And it's no trouble to me.'
They splashed into the yard of the farm.

Mary appeared at the farmhouse door before they
had a chance to get out of the car. A slight, bent
figure in a traditional pinny—Nikki had never seen
her wear anything else on the farm. 'I've got the
kettle on,' Mary called.

'It's only a week since I've seen her,' Nikki whispered, 'and she looks thinner than ever.'

'Her face looks tired. I want to examine her as
well as George.'

Nikki got out of the car and reached for the groceries on the back seat. 'This is Dr Murray, Mary.
Why don't you take him in to see George? I'll unload
these things and make the tea.'

'As you like, Nikki. Welcome to Greystone Farm,
Dr Murray. You're not from round here, are you?
Where do you come from?'

Nikki smiled to herself. Mary dearly loved a gossip—she saw too few people out here.

She took the groceries into the stone-floored
kitchen. In fact, the entire ground floor was laid in
stone. It might be authentic—but it was bitterly cold
in winter. As ever, there was the kettle boiling on
the range. She made the tea, set the tray, complete

with a little traycloth—Mary would never forgive her if she left it off—and carried it through.

They had converted a side room into a bedroom on the ground floor. George spent most of his time here. Now he was sitting on a chair next to the bed, his glasses on the table, a large-print volume of Dickens next to it. George didn't watch TV—reception was poor in the valley anyway. George read Dickens. And when he'd finished it all, he re-read it.

First there was the ritual cup of tea to be drunk, and Nikki had to relay all the gossip about the neighbours. Then Tom said, 'I've had a look at George and we've had a chat. There doesn't seem to be much change. We'll keep up the treatment as before, the analgesics and the anti-inflammatories. I'm afraid there's not much more we can do. But what I'd like to do now is have a look at you, Mary.'

'There's no need, I'm all right,' Mary said sharply. 'George is the ill one.'

Nikki caught Tom's quick glance. He needed support. 'I do think it'd be a good idea to let the doctor examine you, Mary,' she said. 'We can't have you getting ill too, can we?'

'No chance of that. I haven't been ill in the last forty years and I'm not going to start now.' But she allowed herself to be persuaded to go upstairs and let Tom look at her. Nikki accompanied them.

'You're very healthy for your age, 'Tom said after he'd examined her. 'Pulse, BP, heart all seem to be quite strong. Now I'm going to ask Nikki to take a blood sample before we go and I'd like you to give her a urine specimen. But I don't anticipate any organic trouble. Tell me, how does George feel first thing in the morning?'

Nikki had to admire Tom's skill. Apparently casually, he drew out the full story—of how Mary worked all day and much of the night to keep George happy and comfortable. Even Nikki hadn't realised quite how hard Mary worked.

'How long since you had a holiday?' Tom asked finally.

Mary laughed. 'Holiday? What's that? I don't need a holiday. I stay here and look after my husband.'

'Let's go and see him again,' said Tom. 'And I'd love another cup of tea.'

George looked up anxiously as they filed into his room again. 'Is Mary all right?'

'She's fine,' said Tom. 'Physically in very good shape.' He accepted the cup of tea that Mary handed him. 'But you're right, she's tired, I think she needs a rest. She needs to be looked after and cosseted and have an easy life for a week or so. She needs a respite.'

He turned to Mary. 'I've talked about this with George, Mary, and we both agree. You need a rest. We could arrange for George to go into a respite home for a few days and you could do nothing but—'

Mary's cup crashed into its saucer. 'No,' she said, 'my place is here at home with my husband. I don't want a holiday and he's not going to any nursing home.'

'Mary, you need a rest,' said Tom quietly. 'You're pushing yourself too hard. We can arrange somewhere really fine for George.'

'I think it's a great idea,' George joined in. 'Mary, you're getting thinner every day. I'm worried about you, love.'

'He would like a change,' said Nikki. 'We could get him in at Ghyllhead Nursing Home—the head nurse there is Agnes Garthwaite's daughter. She'll look after George really well.'

'I've looked after George for the past fifty years and I see no reason to stop now. George isn't moving. That's final, that's the end of it. George stays here.'

'Well, at least think about it,' Nikki said soothingly. 'There's no need to make any sudden decisions. But you will think about it, Mary, won't you?'

'She'll think about it,' said George. 'I'll talk to her about it. I think it's a grand idea.' A look from his wife silenced him.

Tom and Nikki left shortly afterwards, Tom shaking hands and promising to call in again soon. 'We— I suppose that means you—will have to put pressure on Mary,' he said once they were back in Nikki's four-wheel-drive. 'You know she's headed for a breakdown, don't you?'

'Yes, I know it. And I think a fortnight's respite would be a great thing for her. Incidentally, you got further with her than I ever have. But pressure is the last thing she needs. She loves her husband. She may be stubborn but it's love that drives her. And I think that's wonderful.'

He glanced at her and smiled. 'You have values, beliefs, and you don't mind talking about them, do you?' he said. 'I think that's wonderful, but Mary's love is making her ill. And unhappy. It can happen that way. You're loved by someone and you feel guilty because you're going to cause them pain.'

It was said in an odd voice and it made Nikki wonder. Choosing her words carefully, she said,

'You sound as if you know something about this kind of situation. Something personal? Is it something you've experienced?'

He laughed. 'No, not really, it's just a little observation.' Before she could push him further he went on, 'You seem to get on with them very well. Did you know them before you became their nurse?'

'I've known them years! When I was a little girl I worked on their farm when they were haymaking. My parents live in the next valley, I was born over there.'

'So close? You didn't say. Can we call in? I've got time to if you have.'

A great burst of pleasure welled up inside her. Tom wanted to meet her parents. That was good, she wanted them to meet him. 'Are you sure you want to?' she asked.

'Of course. I wouldn't have asked otherwise. But if you think it's a bad time…'

'No! Not at all!' She glanced at her watch and then reached forward to switch on the little device that enabled her to use her mobile phone without taking her hands off the steering wheel. 'Dad? Where's Ma? What are you doing inside on a day like this?'

Her father's deep voice echoed round her car. 'Your mother's getting ready to go out and I'm doing a bit of book-keeping. Where are you?'

'Well, I'm handy. I've just been to see George and Mary. I was going to ask if you could cope with two more for lunch, but if Ma is—'

'You just get here, love, and your mother will hang on to see you before she goes out. Then you can have some bread and cheese. Did you say two for lunch?'

'I'm bringing a friend. See you, Dad.'

Nikki rang off and turned to Tom. 'Lunch is arranged.'

'Sounds good. In fact, it sounds more than good. Tell me a bit about your family.'

Again she thought that it was unusual that he wanted to meet her parents. Most men didn't—well, not straight away.

'We've always lived here. We can trace our family back hundreds of years and sometimes I think we know everybody within a twenty-mile radius. Family, friends, enemies even…they're all here. I'm the youngest of three—I've got two older brothers who are married and have children of their own.'

'And all live locally?'

'Of course.' She smiled. 'Now, fair's fair, tell me about your family.' She thought for a moment and added, 'If you want to, that is.'

He was silent for a while then he said, 'There's very little to tell. I have no family. My father died before I was born—he was an engineer, killed in some kind of works accident. I can just remember my mother, but she died when I was quite young. I was brought up by my mother's sister. She was much older than my mother and never married. But she did her best by me and she died just after I'd got into medical school.'

She looked at him in horror. 'Tom! That's a terrible story!'

'Not really. It makes you…self-sufficient. Now I have a handful of friends in London, most of them medical people. As you climb the ladder, you tend to work hard and move around a lot. Not a good atmosphere for making long-lasting relationships.'

'Not the kind of life that would do for me,' Nikki said.

'Sometimes it has its compensations.'

She thought this an odd thing to say and was going to ask more but they'd come to the entrance to High Walls Farm. There was that constriction of the throat that she always felt when she came back to the place where she'd been born and lived so happily. Her mother and father came out to greet them.

There was only time for quick introductions and then her mother had to go into town—a committee meeting of some sort. Her mother was an expert organiser and on dozens of committees. Nikki caught the calm but assessing look her mother gave Tom. They only talked for five minutes, but Nikki knew that her mother would have found out more about Tom than he ever realised. 'I do hope we meet again quite soon,' she said to him. 'Get Nikki to bring you to tea.' And then she was gone.

Nikki thought her father and Tom would get on. They were the same physical type, though her father was burned red-brown by sun and wind and his body was bulky compared with Tom's sinewy leanness. But both seemed the same kind of man.

She watched them shaking hands, looking, sizing each other up, being a little guarded in their first exchanges. They're both wondering about what the other means to me, she realised, and the thought gave her great pleasure.

They went to the kitchen to eat. It was warm from the solid fuel stove at one end which burned summer and winter alike. Unlike George's and Mary's house, wooden floors had been laid over the old stones.

Her mother baked every second day. There was

fresh bread, local cheese and a bowl of salad on the table. They sat and started to eat, and Nikki told her father about George and Mary. Then she said anxiously to Tom, 'This isn't breaking medical confidentiality. Dad and George are old friends and Dad goes over there when he can. He needs to know how things are.'

'Seems like the best kind of medicine to me,' said Tom.

He was just telling her father what he liked about being in the country when the phone rang. Her father answered, listened for a while and then said, 'Be right over, Ben. Give me half an hour.'

To Nikki and Tom he explained, 'That was Ben Castleton. He was haymaking and his haymaker's broken down. He can't fix it but he thinks I can. He's panicking, he's got two more fields to gather in and he thinks it might rain tomorrow.'

'You go and get changed,' said Nikki. 'I'll make you a couple of sandwiches and a flask of tea. You can eat on your way.'

As her father went to change she explained to Tom, 'You cut your hay and wait for it to dry, then you gather it in for winter feed. But if it rains when it's been cut and has to dry out again, it loses half of its goodness.'

'I didn't realise farming was such a gamble,' said Tom.

Her father came back down, shook hands again and said he didn't want to appear inhospitable and he hoped to see Tom again very soon. And then he was gone.

'Your father didn't hesitate,' reflected Tom. 'He went off to help his friend just like that.'

'It's the way we are round here. Ben Castleton would have done the same for Dad.'

'Hmm. You're very like your father, aren't you?'

She was intrigued by this. 'I didn't think so. People say my mother looks more like me.'

'I didn't mean in looks. There's something about your character. Now, what's it like, growing up in a place like this? What's it like in winter?'

For a while they chatted about her early life. They ate—she noticed that although he obviously enjoyed his food he didn't eat much.

Tom looked out of the deep-alcoved window at the hill that rose behind the farm. 'It must be wonderful to see that from your bedroom window. All I could ever see were chimneys.'

'I grew up looking at Cragend Hill. I remember the first day I walked up it myself. I thought after that that I could do anything. Strange childhood ideas I had.'

'Not really. I think it's a pity when you have to rein in your ambitions, let the dreary world limit what you want to do.' He looked at her thoughtfully. 'How soon do you have to be back?'

She hadn't expected this. 'Any time that suits me. I've got four calls left to make today. It's up to me when I make them. Why?'

'I've got the afternoon off. Would you take me to the top of your hill? I want to see where you thought you could do anything.'

All sorts of odd thoughts swirled round her brain. 'All right,' she said. 'I'll find you a pair of boots to wear.'

They set off ten minutes later. It was a pilgrimage for her, she hadn't climbed this hill for five or six years. But what was it for Tom? 'Why d'you really want to come up here?' Nikki asked.

It took him a couple of minutes of pondering before he could answer. 'It's a bit like playing truant. I've got the afternoon off, but perhaps there are things I should be doing. I would never have taken time out like this in London. But I came up here to do the things that I've never had time for before. And then there's you. I want to see the top of the hill that inspired you so much.'

'I was only eight,' she said. 'And my mother packed me a bottle of lemonade and a cheese sandwich.'

'Your mother sent you on an adventure when you were eight. That was nice.'

Something about his tone made her ask, 'How old were you when your mother died, Tom?'

'I was eight.' A simple, flat statement.

'Oh. I'm sorry, I didn't know. I didn't mean to hurt you.'

'You didn't,' Tom said gently. 'I was feeling happy for you. Now, where do we go after this stile?'

They climbed the stile and followed the path along the side of a wall, ascending steadily. Rather to her surprise, she was a better walker than he was. She had to slow down her natural pace and was breathing easily when he was out of breath.

'I'm not very fit,' he confessed. 'I need to do a lot more walking.'

'A few weeks working out here and you'll be walking like a shepherd. Now, another couple of hundred yards and we'll be at the summit.'

The last few yards were the easiest. Like most of the hills round there, the summit was nearly flat.

Only a cairn of stones marked the highest point, and when they reached the cairn Nikki carefully added a stone to it. It was tradition—that way the cairn never got worn away. Then they looked round. 'What do you think of the view?' she asked.

Nikki had often seen it, but it still filled her with wonder. In all directions there were moors. In the distance there was even a glimpse of the Irish Sea. There were farms, villages and small towns dotted on the all-embracing greenery. It was amazing.

Tom said nothing, just looked. Slowly he turned, staring into the distance in each direction. She couldn't read his expression, a longing, a yearning for something perhaps—but what?

Then he turned to her and she knew he was going to kiss her.

He kissed her with such searing intensity, such urgency and desperation that she didn't know what to make of it. She responded to his hunger, clutching him to her with the same bone-crushing intensity. The full length of her body was pressed to his and she felt that he could know her, feel her very essence even though they were both fully clothed.

The kiss might have lasted for minutes, it might have lasted for hours, but eventually his head lifted from hers and she saw him stare into the distance again. There was no way she could read what was in those unfathomable green eyes.

High above them, a curlew called. A distant mournful cry.

There was no need for words. In fact, there were no words to express what she felt. Her mind was in turmoil. Between them something had happened— but what? A kiss that had showed such passion—

surely he couldn't just let it go, surely he would have
to say something? But apparently not. The arms that
had held her so tightly now relaxed and he stroked
her back gently, as if soothing her.

Then he did try to speak. 'Nikki,' he began, 'I
didn't mean that to happen, but it did and now
we…well, we…'

'Please, I don't want to talk,' she said softly. 'I
don't want to think either, I just want to feel.'

'Yes,' he said. 'That's all I want to do.'

'But you felt what I did?'

It was a while before he spoke. 'Yes. I think I felt
exactly the same.'

After a while, still without speaking, they set off
down the hill, but this time they held hands. It was
a small thing, but it made her feel part of him. Her
father still hadn't returned when they got back to the
farm so she left him a note and they drove back
towards Hambleton.

Her mind was still whirling so she sought refuge
in everyday things. 'I've got a couple of calls in town
I ought to make,' she said. 'A phlebotomy and a
young diabetic I want to check up on. Shall I drop
you off at the White House?'

'Yes, please,' Tom replied. 'There are things that
I ought to do as well.'

He didn't seem to be about to say any more, but
she felt that she couldn't just let what had happened
go without comment. 'We'll have to talk some time,'
she said, 'but there's no mad rush. Would you like
to come to tea tonight? Nothing fancy—sandwiches
or something on toast. If it's still warm we can eat
out on the patio.'

'Dining with you? I like that. Yes, Nikki, I'd love

to come to tea. About seven? But I'll have to get back quite quickly—I've got some bookwork I have to check up on.'

'That's fine,' she said. To herself she thought it quite a good idea. Perhaps she needed to keep a clear head.

They pulled up outside the White House. Tom got out quickly and then leaned through the open window to say, 'You know Nikki, I'll never forget that walk with you. Not till the day I die.' And then he was gone.

Rather a cheerless way of putting things, Nikki thought, but it was a nice compliment. And she suspected she felt as he did.

Nikki decided that she'd do as she'd suggested— have a very simple tea. So she cooked scrambled eggs on toast and put a salad to the side. Tom came promptly at seven to join her. After tea she made him sit outside while she hastily washed up, and then they sat side by side in the late evening warmth.

'Seeing your mother and father, seeing the place you were born and grew up, it had an odd effect on me,' he said. 'It made you seem more real, more a proper person, whereas I'm rootless. I belong no-where, to no one.'

'You can put down roots if you want. A lot of medical people feel like you—they've given their lives to their work. Things will change as time passes.'

'Possibly.' He stared upwards at the greenery of the oak tree that shaded her caravan. 'How long have I known you, Nikki?'

She calculated. 'You dropped into my life a week

last Saturday—dropped out of the sky, it seemed. I've known you less than a week. It seems longer. It feels like I've known you for ever.'

'I know. I feel the same.' He wouldn't look at her, kept staring at the tree.

She'd never been someone who avoided a confrontation. 'There seems to be something troubling you, Tom. Will you tell me what it is? I think you owe me that.'

He sighed. 'Yes, I do owe you that.' Then he looked at her directly and she was surprised at the pain in his eyes. 'It's us, Nikki. We're moving too fast. I came here to have a year out, to think about things and look about me a bit. I met you and it's been wonderful. But we've got to slow down a little.'

'If you find something or someone that you like, you go for it,' she said. 'That's how I've always been.'

He laughed. 'Don't I know it. Nikki, please, believe me, I'm thinking of you. I don't want you to be disappointed or made unhappy. I…like you a lot and I want to see more of you. But I don't want things to get too intense.'

She had to ask. 'There isn't another woman in your life, is there? Just tell me and we'll forget everything and just be pals.'

'No. There's no woman in my life. I have had relationships but there's no one—absolutely no one—who has any kind of claim on me now.'

She was sure he was sincere. 'All right, then. Where do we go from here?'

'We keep things calm. We see each other, work together. We're friends as well as colleagues. We'll have a fun relationship.'

'Is that what you want? Tell me truly, Tom, please.'

He didn't answer at first. She thought he looked disturbed. Then he said, 'We could have a relationship—perhaps even a physical one. Something that lasted a few weeks, perhaps a few months and then ended with no hard feelings. But you deserve better than that and I don't think that I could be happy with it either. You would mean too much to me. And what we have to remember is that in a very short time I'll be gone.'

It seemed very strange to Nikki, but now wasn't the time to argue. 'All right,' she said, 'we'll do as you say. But remember—I'll fight for what I want.'

'I know that. And if I'd met you a year ago...'

He stood, bent over and kissed her gently. 'Thanks for tea but I must go now. Bookwork to do. You've no idea what you mean to me, Nikki.' And he was gone.

It had been an odd day, she thought. She couldn't make sense of it. That kiss on the hilltop—it had altered her life. But now Tom was saying that all he wanted was a fun relationship. She was certain—as certain as she'd been of anything in her life—that the kiss had meant the same to him. And what had he meant when he said he wished he'd met her a year ago?

One thing was certain. She felt more for Tom than she'd ever felt for a man before. Was he the one she'd been half expecting?

Nikki didn't see Tom over the weekend. There was no sign of him at the White House, and when she casually asked Joe about him on Monday she was told that Dr Murray had gone to Leeds for a few days.

'There's a case at the hospital there that he's interested in,' Joe said gruffly. 'We agreed when he started that there might be the odd time when he'd be called down there. I said we'd work round it.'

'Seems a bit odd,' Nikki said. 'I thought he worked in London.'

'Cases can be transferred.' Joe picked up a folder, looked at it and threw it back on his desk in irritation. 'I'm not sure having a London doctor here was such a good idea after all. He'll be disturbing everyone. And the minute we get used to him he'll be gone again.'

'He's a good doctor, the patients like him. So do I.'

'Just so long as you don't get too fond of him. He'll be out of your life soon enough.'

There it was again. A warning about Tom. Nikki felt irritated and was about to challenge Joe, but thought better of it. She knew the older doctor had her best interests at heart.

CHAPTER FOUR

IT WAS too bad that her first call that afternoon was to old Mrs Ravensby. Mrs Ravensby was an eighty-one-year-old widow who lived alone in a tiny terraced house near the church. She steadfastly refused to move in with either her son or her daughter, who both lived out in the suburbs. Mrs Ravensby needed to observe, to be at the centre of things.

Nikki called twice a week to dress the ulcers on Mrs Ravensby's legs. If the old lady used her legs less the ulcers might have a better chance of healing, but at least three times a day Mrs Ravensby needed to walk down the high street, to talk to friends and acquaintances, to watch, to make sure she missed nothing.

'He's nice, that new doctor,' the old lady said as Nikki carefully sprinkled powder on the angry-looking weal on her thigh, 'He told me you might try some new ointment. I went to see him last week you know.'

Mrs Ravensby visited the surgery once a fortnight, whether ill or not.

'He told me. He also said that you ought to relax more to give these ulcers a chance to heal.'

This wasn't what Mrs Ravensby wanted to hear, so she ignored it. 'Can't understand why he isn't married,' she said, raising her eyebrows. 'A doctor should be married. Then he'd know about…things.'

Nikki decided not to ask what 'things'. 'A lot of

doctors don't get married till late in their careers,' she said.

'Well, they ought to. Now, in my day—'

'That's your leg finished,' Nikki interrupted. 'I'm sorry but I really must fly now. See you next week?' She knew that once they were started on how things were in Mrs. Ravensby's day, a couple of hours could pass.

'All right, then, next week. Thank you, Nikki. And you ought to be married yourself, you know. You're not a young girl any more, all the men will be snapped up. And then you'll never—'

Nikki wondered with horror if she was going to be told that she'd never know all about 'things'.

'I'll find a man in time,' she said. 'There must be a Mr Right waiting for me somewhere. Bye, Mrs Ravensby. I'll let myself out.' And she was gone.

As she drove to her next appointment she thought that she hadn't really wanted to be told that it was time she got married.

When Nikki got back to her caravan the next evening there was a thick envelope for her in the post. She knew what it was—tickets for the annual Farmers' Midsummer Ball. She opened the envelope and tapped the invitations thoughtfully on the table.

This was the biggest local social event of the year. She went every year—and always enjoyed it. It had been the first ever ball she had gone to. She'd been seventeen, in her first long dress which her mother had made her. It had been magic then and it had been magic ever since.

She would need a new dress this time. She would also need a partner.

Even as she thought this, something flashed in the corner of her eye. She looked across at the White House. A light had just come on in the kitchen at the back. Tom was back home.

She remembered their last conversation and wondered if she was being forward again. Then she decided she wasn't. Besides, they were neighbours. Steeling herself, she walked across the lawn and knocked on his back door, clutching the tickets.

'You must have been working hard in Leeds.' She smiled when he answered the door, 'You look tired.'

Tom smiled back wearily. 'You know what medicine is like. It can take it out of you.' He hesitated and then said, 'Why don't you come in?' Not exactly the warmest of welcomes.

He seemed ill at ease, as if he wasn't happy having her in his kitchen. Perhaps he was very tired. Perhaps he had some urgent plan and didn't want to be disturbed. Nikki decided to rush on with the reason for her visit although it would have been nice to gossip for a while.

She held up her tickets. 'I've just got my tickets to the Farmers' Midsummer Ball,' she said. 'It's the biggest event in the Hambleton social calendar. Everyone dresses up in their best or hires something. I always go.' She didn't like the distant way he was looking at her so her last few words came out in a rush. 'Would you like to come as my partner?'

There was a silence that seemed to stretch on and on. Then he said flatly, 'I'm sorry, but I've already accepted an invitation, Nikki. Meriel McCarthy phoned me this morning and invited me to be her partner. I said I'd go with her.'

There was another silence. Eventually she said,

'Goodness, you are getting to know the local people fast, aren't you? I'm glad…I'm glad you're fitting in so well. I guess I'll see you there, then.'

She could say no more. She stared down at the kitchen table, not wanting to look up at him, not wanting him to know what she was feeling.

But, of course, he did know. 'I did tell you that all we should have was a fun relationship, Nikki. I do like you a lot. But you belong here and I…I belong nowhere. After a year I'll be gone…back to where I came from. There can't be anything between us, I told you that. We're just going to be good friends.'

Her voice cracked, she couldn't take any more. 'If you just wanted to be good friends then you shouldn't have kissed me that way on Cragend Hill. That was wrong of you!' She was horrified to feel the sting of tears in her eyes.

'I know that. It was very wrong. I can only say that I'm sorry.'

'I'm sorry, too.' Nikki fought for control. 'But we'll do what you want. And, yes, we'll stay friends. Just tell me one thing. Is being my friend all you really want? You've got to be honest with me, Tom!' She took his arm, pulled him round so he had to meet her eyes.

He wouldn't look at her. 'I think it's better this way,' he said after a while.

'As you wish. I'm going back to my caravan now. Goodbye, Tom.'

She turned and stumbled out of the kitchen.

Once back in her caravan Nikki opened a bottle of wine, sat there and drank a glass. Then she put the cork back in the bottle and the bottle back in the fridge. She would have one glass. There was no way she would turn into the kind of woman who had to drown her sorrows in alcohol. She'd seen too much of that.

She'd really thought that Tom was going to be the man for her. She'd felt more for him than any other man she'd ever met. And didn't he know what kind of girl Meriel McCarthy was? Desolate, she realised that wasn't fair. Meriel was certainly a flirt, but she had a good heart. She would never willingly hurt anyone.

Thoroughly disheartened, Nikki finished her glass of wine. She thought of fetching the bottle from the fridge. Then she did some paperwork instead.

Saturday morning. How many Saturdays since Tom had fallen onto her roof? Only three, just a fortnight. It seemed like an age. So much seemed to have happened. Her life had changed quite definitely and… No, her life hadn't changed. She had seen nothing of Tom for the past four days, and that was the best way. Friends didn't need to see each other all that often. Not like lovers.

She would go into town, change her library books, get a few groceries, probably find someone to gossip to. A relaxed, pleasant morning, a change from the racing around typical of her work days. She would take things easy—but she wouldn't brood on things that couldn't be altered.

In fact, she had just finished a satisfying chat with a farmer friend in the main street when she saw a figure she recognised. She was surprised, a little upset at the shock it gave her. It was Tom—dressed, as so often, in black.

He hadn't seen her. He was walking purposefully to the church that stood at the end of the street. Under his arm was a long thin package. What was Tom doing in church? Well, it was no business of hers. She slipped into the library, her next errand. But she couldn't concentrate on picking out books, and soon left without taking any. What was Tom doing in church? He'd never shown any interest before.

She could have gone into the Kozy Kafé for a drink, there certainly would be someone there to talk to, but instead she paused and then walked up to the church. After all, they were supposed to be friends. Friends said hello.

St Mary's was a fine church, built centuries ago when Hambleton had been a thriving wool town, one of the richest in the North. It stood in the town centre, raised above it, its red stone steeple visible for miles. When she had time Nikki sang in the choir. One day Nikki thought, hoped, she would get… What was Tom doing in there?

Behind her, the door thudded softly shut. Sunlight spread across the pews, coloured by the ancient leaded windows. It was serene in here, she felt calmed. But there was no sign of Tom—the church appeared to be deserted. Well, perhaps he'd left while she'd been in the library. No matter, she would sit here a while anyway.

Then she heard a rustle, which appeared to be coming from the side aisle. But she could see no one. Curious, she walked over. And there was Tom, on his hands and knees, rubbing industriously at a sheet of gold paper that was stretched across the floor. 'What are you doing?' she asked.

He looked up, surprised to hear her voice, but by

his smile she thought he was pleased to see her. Though there was a sadness there too, as if his pleasure was in some way wrong. If he was so pleased to see her, why hadn't he…? Stop thinking that way!

Still smiling, he said, 'Hello, Nikki, good to see you. Look, I'm rubbing this brass.' He lifted a corner of the gold paper and underneath she could see the dull outline of a memorial brass fastened to the top of a huge stone slab. She had seen it before—knew vaguely that it was considered quite good of its kind—but had never looked at it with any great interest. It was in a dark and little visited area of the church.

Tom held some kind of black crayon and was rubbing it across the gold paper so that the lines of the brass showed through. She saw the heads and faces of the couple—a crusader and his wife. The crusader wore a helmet of chain mail and his wife a wimple.

'I didn't know you were into brass rubbing,' she said, her voice remaining steady.

'I've never done it before. But it's calming, it's satisfying and it's something completely new for me. I came up here to change my life, and this is part of the change.'

He leaned back so she could see more clearly what he was doing. 'Now look at the faces of these two people. I've only just started, this is all I've done.'

For the first time she looked closely. It was a simple line drawing and yet as she looked it seemed to get more complicated.

'What are they both thinking?' Tom asked softly. 'I've been rubbing away here, watching these two faces appear, and I want to know what they're thinking.'

Nikki stared downwards. 'I've never really looked before,' she said. 'But I suppose they were…in love?' Her words seemed to echo through the church.

'Yes,' he said after a while, 'I think you're right, they were in love. And that love has lasted through the centuries. Will love today last so long? Rather thought-provoking isn't it?'

'Yes.' Suddenly she had difficulty speaking.

Now he wasn't looking up at her but down at the two faces. 'And she has this lovely heart-shaped face,' he went on. 'It reminds me just a bit of yours.'

It hadn't been meant as a compliment, she realised, but a simple statement of fact. She looked even harder—and, yes, perhaps there was a slight resemblance. 'I can see what you mean,' she said, her mouth dry. 'And…I suppose it's not impossible…my family has been here for years.'

He nodded. 'Your roots are here, it's something I envy you.'

She didn't know what more to say. What had started as a polite exchange had suddenly turned into something deeper.

He offered her a crayon. 'Would you like to try? You could start at the feet, work upwards. We could meet in the middle.'

For a moment Nikki was tempted. 'I'm sorry, I'd like to, but I've got to meet someone. Perhaps some other time.' Then, thinking that she perhaps had sounded unfriendly, she added, 'But I'd like to see the finished result.'

'I'll bring it over to show you.'

He seemed quite happy to leave his work and to chat to her but she knew she had to go. 'See you, then, Tom,' she said, and fled. Looking back, she saw him watching after her. Then he bent to his rubbing again. Good. She didn't want him to know just how much his remarks about ever-lasting love had affected her.

As soon as she'd walked back to the caravan, she packed an overnight bag and drove out to her parents' farm. She stayed there till late Sunday night. That way Tom couldn't just drop in to see her. They were friends, of course, but she didn't want to see his rubbing of a love that had lasted for centuries. She was more interested in a love that might last just for a lifetime. Unfortunately, he wasn't.

As usual, Nikki called into the surgery on Monday morning to check her mail, pick up her medicines and find if there were any new calls. Joe caught her just as she was leaving again.

'Nikki, I had a phone call this morning from Alice Lowe. She thinks that that son of hers hasn't been taking his tablets. He says he has, but he won't take them in front of her. He's getting aggressive, too. I asked her to get him to come in, but she says he refuses.'

'We've had trouble like this before,' Nikki said.

'I know. Perhaps we ought to get him into hospital again but if we can persuade him...' Joe sighed. 'You don't have to go if you're busy.'

'I'll drop in at the end of the morning. We were at school together, perhaps there's something I can help him with.'

'Yes, well...be careful, Nikki. These mood changes can be quite violent.'

'Toby and I go back a long way. I'll be all right.' She wished she was as confident as she sounded.

When she remembered Toby as he once was—a shy young man, ever ready to help anyone—she felt she could weep.

Toby lived with his mother in a pleasant semi on the outskirts of town. He was in—but his mother said that he spent most of his time up in his room.

'He lost that job he had,' Alice said sadly. 'Freddy Hanley took him on at the farm, working on the machinery and so on. But he had to let him go. It wasn't Freddy's fault, he felt really bad about it, but the farm owner said he couldn't afford another hand. There was nothing wrong with Toby's work. But he doesn't see it that way. He thinks that everyone is against him. And since the middle of last week it's got worse.'

'I'll just go up and see how he is,' said Nikki reassuringly. 'If he's really not taking his medication, that's bad and we need to sort it out.'

It was also, she knew, quite common. Some people just forgot to take drugs. Others, especially those suffering from mental conditions, thought that they were cured and that there was no need for further medication. And then there were those who refused to take their drugs as a punishment to their families, to the medical profession, to the world in general. She thought Toby fell into the last category.

He didn't answer when Nikki knocked and called out his name, so she walked in anyway. It was like a teenager's room, with the walls covered with pictures of the motorbikes he could no longer ride. From what she could see, Toby hadn't shaved for three or four days. She suspected he hadn't washed either. Toby was in a mess.

The room echoed with the sound of an engine. He

was staring at a screen, jerking a small steering-wheel to and fro, apparently playing some kind of computer game which involved driving a car round a racing track. He didn't look up as she walked in and carried on with his game.

'Just thought I'd drop in,' said Nikki brightly, 'How are you, Toby?'

He didn't answer but carried on with his game. Then there was a screech and apparently an accident. In a temper, he threw the controller on the bed.

'You made me crash! Now I have to start again!'

'Sorry, Toby. I just wanted to—'

'I know what you want and I haven't got the time.'

'If that's the way you feel, I'll go,' she said.

She was almost out of the door before he called her back—as she'd calculated he would. Toby wanted attention. 'I don't know why you want to talk to me. No one else bothers with me. I've got no friends, no job and I get these lousy headaches.'

'The headaches wouldn't be as bad if you took your drugs. Your mother's worried about you.'

'Let her worry.' At least now that he'd put down the steering-wheel, he was giving her his attention.

'Why not switch off that machine and talk to me a minute?' Nikki said gently. 'We can talk about things, can't we? Is there something special bothering you?'

It was a while before she managed to draw it out of him. Toby might have been ill but he still had his pride. Eventually, he confessed. 'It's the Farmers' Ball,' he said moodily. 'I've been there every year since I was sixteen. I was really looking forward to it. And this year I'm going to have to go on my own. I've asked three girls to go with me and they've all said no, though I know they don't have partners. What's wrong with me?'

It wasn't what Nikki would have wanted, but Toby was an old friend and he was in trouble. For that matter, she was in trouble herself. She wanted to go to the Farmers' Ball and it was much more fun with a partner.

She thought for a minute, then said, 'I'm not going with anyone, Toby. You could go with me if you like. You know, just two old pals going together for a laugh.'

He looked at her, obviously amazed. 'But what about that new doctor? I've seen you around with him. Why isn't he taking you?'

He didn't know how much he was hurting her— why should he? Managing to stay calm, Nikki said, 'He's just a friend, Toby. And, besides, he's taking Meriel McCarthy.'

'That's great!' Now he knew she meant it, Toby was obviously overjoyed. 'We can start by going to dinner at the—'

'No dinner, Toby.' What she was about to say wasn't strictly true but she wanted to be kind to him. 'I'll be working that day till the last possible minute.'

The next thing was to work out the best way of not allowing Toby to have any illusions about them. She didn't want to raise his hopes, that would be cruel. 'This isn't a date,' she said as kindly but as clearly as she could. 'We're two old friends going to a dance together. I'll expect to dance with other people, I'll expect you to do the same. We'll just be pals, like we've always been. Okay?'

Now there was nothing Toby wouldn't do for her. 'Sure, Nikki, no problem. Just two old friends.'

Perhaps this was the right time to press her advantage. 'And you will start taking your pills and carry on with them? You really need them, you know.'

'No problem! I've only missed...say a day or two.'

Nikki privately thought it was probably more but she said nothing about it. 'And, of course, you don't drink—not anything. You know how alcohol doesn't mix with your pills. You can do it for us both, Toby. Then we'll have a great time.'

'You say it, I'll do it. Nikki, I feel better already!'

Nikki watched as he swallowed his pills and then went down to tell his mother that Toby was in a slightly better mood. Then she set off on her rounds, rather gloomily. This wasn't the way she'd envisaged going to the ball. Then she thought of the pleasure so obvious in Toby's face and felt guilty. At least it was good to help your friends if you could.

Just under another fortnight later it was the night of the ball. Saturday night. Recently, her life seemed to have been marked by Saturdays. She had met Tom for the first time on a Saturday, a fortnight later had seen him rub a brass, now another fortnight had passed and they would be meeting at the ball. She made herself cheer up. There would be old friends there, the food was always good, the music better. She would have a good time—if it killed her. And when she saw Tom there, well, she would greet him like the friend he was. No way was he to see that she was suffering.

She hadn't bought a new dress, she really hadn't had the heart for it. Instead, she wore a long silver-grey sheath, split to the thigh, which she had worn only twice before. She knew she looked well and that it emphasised her good points—her long legs and slim figure. Tom would see what he was missing.

Toby had said that if they weren't going to dinner, at least he would pick her up. She had persuaded him not to by saying she had promised to share a taxi with a couple of receptionists from the surgery. They would all meet at the Tinsley Arms, with everyone else. Toby had accepted this.

There were perhaps thirty people in the back room—all in their dinner jackets or their long dresses. Toby saw her, waved and walked over. He gave her a glass of the white wine that she liked and lifted his own glass. 'Grapefruit juice and tonic,' he said proudly. Then he looked around. 'Isn't it good to be with so many old friends, Nikki? I'm glad we could go together.' Again she felt a little ashamed of her earlier doubts.

She knew most of the people there and was introduced to those she didn't know. She and Toby moved from group to group, chatting and reminiscing. There was no sign of Tom or Meriel. Nikki was glad about that.

Finally the entire group walked over to the Assembly Rooms. They looked colourful crossing the road, she thought, the men's dark suits setting off the women's bright outfits. The sun was still shining, making them look like an exotic flock of tropical birds.

As always, the committee had done a good job. Bright swathes of white and gold cloth stretched down the walls from the ceiling, making it appear that they were dancing in a vast oriental tent. The floor had always been good for dancing. Toby found the table allocated to them and she decided to relax.

'There's that doctor I saw you with,' Toby said suddenly.

She looked up and saw Tom, was shocked at the pain it gave her. Like all the men, he was wearing a dinner jacket—but there was a sheen about his that suggested it was made from something different from the serviceable wool of the other men's. The whiteness of his shirt emphasised his high cheekbones. Tom looked good.

And, Nikki had reluctantly to admit, Meriel was a worthy partner. Her hair had been expensively styled and she wore a classic white ballgown. They made a handsome couple. Meriel caught Nikki looking at her, gave a little wave. Nikki felt depressed. Meriel was obviously loving this.

The dance was starting.

Sometimes she danced with Toby, sometimes she danced with other old friends. Couples they knew came and sat at their table, continuing the gossip from earlier. At times she had to ease Toby off a little. When he danced he tried to hold her just a bit too possessively, too closely. Still, she could deal with it. She decided that, on the whole, she was enjoying herself. And then, suddenly, Tom was at her table.

'Hello, Nikki—and Toby, isn't it? I'm Tom Murray.' She saw Toby reluctantly take the offered hand.

'Tom.' He nodded stiffly.

'If you don't mind, I'd like to ask your partner for a dance,' Tom said formally.

'Well, I was just—'

'I'd love to dance with you, Tom,' Nikki said swiftly. 'Toby knows that we're here to dance with as many people as we can. Don't you, Toby?'

She knew there was steel in her voice, but she'd guessed that Toby had been about to object. She and Toby had an agreement, an understanding. He would stick to it!

'It's all right, I suppose,' Toby mumbled, and Tom offered her his hand. He seemed to grasp the situation instantly.

It was bliss to dance with Tom. She might have guessed that he would be a good dancer, and for a couple of minutes she gave herself to the pleasure of being with him, being pressed close to him. But then, like an aching tooth that had to be prodded, she had to ask. 'Where's Meriel?'

'Claimed for the moment by another man. I like this idea that you can wander round at will and dance with who you like.'

'Is Meriel equally pleased?'

He grinned at her. 'Nurse Gale, that was just a touch catty—and I like you for it.'

She had to blush. 'Yes, I suppose it was. I'm sorry.' They danced on and there was another period of silence and happiness.

'Are you all right with Toby?' he asked after a while. 'He looked a bit miffed when I asked you to dance and I don't want to spoil your—or his—evening. I remember you told me he was subject to violent mood swings.'

'We've got all that sorted out. A clear pre-dance arrangement about the conditions if I was going to come here with him.' She told Tom about visiting Toby, how he hadn't been taking his medication and that she'd offered to come to the dance with him on the understanding he went back on his medication.

Tom listened in silence and smiled. 'You're a good person, Nikki Gale. A kind person. No one should hurt you.' Then he turned her round and said in a totally different voice, 'I thought you said Toby had promised not to drink.'

'Of course. He can't drink, not with his medication.'

'I think he needs reminding.' Tom turned her so she could see the bar. And there was Toby in a small crowd of the younger men there. He had a large glass in his hand and was apparently trying to drink all its contents in one swig. As she looked there was a cheer from his friends. He had apparently succeeded. Just what she needed.

'Please, Tom, I think I ought to get back to him,' she said. 'I don't want to, but I came with him and I suppose I'm partly responsible for him.'

'You can't be responsible for anyone but yourself,' came the quiet reply. 'I know that. But if you want to go back to your table, I'll take you. Though I don't want to.'

That tiny remark pleased her so much!

By the time Tom had led her back to her table Toby was already there. There was another pint of beer in front of him and a large glass of whisky by its side. He pushed a third glass of white wine towards her.

'You sit down and drink that,' he said aggressively. 'From now on you only dance with me.' He looked at Tom. 'And you can get back to where you came from,' he snapped.

Toby's voice was loud and people at the adjoining

tables looked around. Nikki could feel the silence growing around them and so could Toby. It appeared to anger him.

She saw Tom looking calmly at Toby, at her, trying to appraise the situation. 'Nikki just asked me if we could go and chat with Meriel,' he said cheerfully. 'Why don't you come over, too?'

'Because I don't want to chat with Meriel!'

'Then we'll be back.' Tom took Nikki's arm firmly and led her away.

Behind them there was the sudden squeak of a chair on the floor. 'No, you won't!' she heard Toby shout.

Nikki turned just in time to see Toby throw a punch at the unsuspecting Tom. At the last moment Tom saw what was happening and jerked his head away so that Toby's fist glanced off his cheek. When Toby tried to hit him again Tom just pushed him away. Enraged by now, Toby leapt forward, aimed the wildest of punches. Then he slipped and his fist hit Nikki in the face.

Actually, he didn't hit her too hard but she was unbalanced and staggered backwards and fell full length. Then she lay there, horrified, pushing desperately at her skirt which had ridden up round her thighs. What else could go wrong now?

She saw a bunch of friends pull Toby away, hustle him out of the room. She knew they would look after him—someone would take him home. More friends lifted her to her feet, brushed her down, asked if she was all right.

Meriel come over and asked if she was all right. When Nikki said yes, Meriel put her arm round Tom and urged him away. Tom stood still, looking at

Nikki. 'You go, Tom,' Nikki said. 'I'm fine really, I just slipped.' He looked a while longer then let himself be led across the dance floor.

It had been a small incident, carefully dealt with by her friends. The dance could now go on, no one need be too upset—it was understood that these things sometimes happened. Nikki even managed a smile. What an evening!

CHAPTER FIVE

Cocoa. The world might collapse around her but there was always a friend in cocoa. Her mother had made it when Nikki was a child and its association with comfort and security had never gone away. Nikki loved cocoa.

She had undressed, had a shower, moisturised her face and cleaned her teeth. Now she sat in her dressing-gown and drank cocoa. Perhaps she might marry a mug of cocoa. Throughout the years it had brought her more comfort than any man had.

Things had moved smoothly at the ball after she'd been helped up from the floor. From somewhere Joe had arrived, taken a quick look at her face and decided—as she'd known already—that there had been nothing seriously wrong. Then he'd asked who'd taken Toby home and had quickly left to catch them up. Apparently Tom wasn't hurt either. But her evening had been spoiled and she hadn't wanted to ruin it for anyone else so she'd quietly left. For a start, her dress was dirty. Toby hadn't hurt her, but her dignity had been wounded.

There was a knock on the door and Nikki put down her cocoa. Who could it be at this hour of night? Please, it couldn't be Toby—no, she knew Joe would have taken care of him. More than a few of her friends might call—but the ball was still going on. Whoever it was, she didn't want to know. It was late, she was tired and fed up and wanted to go to bed. 'Who's there?' she shouted rather crossly.

'It's me. Tom. Tom Murray.'

How many Toms did he think she knew? And what did she feel? She couldn't work out what her emotions were. She only knew they were in turmoil.

'What d'you want?' It was a poor, an unwelcoming question but she couldn't think of any other.

'I was worried about you. I saw you get punched and I felt it was my fault.'

She went to open the door, silently gesturing for him to come in and sit opposite her. 'He punched you as well,' she said. 'You could have hit him back.'

He nodded. 'I felt like it. But doctors don't hit men they know to be ill.'

'Some doctors don't.' But she was glad he hadn't hit Toby. She felt it showed an inner strength.

He had changed. Now he was wearing dark jeans and his customary dark shirt. And there was a matching dark bruise on his cheek. Nikki was about to comment when he came round to her side of the little table. He took her head in his hands, looked at her cheek and stroked it. The tips of his fingers trailed down her face and she felt she could sit there and let him stroke her like that for ever.

'It's just bruised,' Tom said tenderly, 'though I bet it hurts. Tomorrow you can cover it with powder.'

'I never use powder,' she told him with the ghost of a smile. 'You don't know much about young women, do you?'

'Evidently not. And I'm finding that learning about them is painful.'

'Where's Meriel?'

'All her family were at the ball so I asked her if she minded if I left her with them. I said I thought I'd better go home, that I didn't feel too good—though I'm afraid that was a bit of a lie.' He was silent a moment and then went on. 'She was quite upset herself. She didn't like to see you lying on the floor like that. And I could tell the others felt the same way.'

'They're my friends,' said Nikki. 'Even Meriel.' Then she asked, 'Why did you lie to her?'

'Because I wanted to come and see you. I knew you were all right—Joe told me—but I still wanted to come and see you.'

'I see,' she said, then added abruptly, 'Would you like a cocoa?'

'I can think of nothing better.'

So she made him one and then raided her biscuit barrel for the last few digestives. They might as well make this a night to remember. Together they ate and drank and she thought her little living room had never seemed so intimate, so friendly.

Perhaps she'd had too much to drink, perhaps it was the reaction from being hit, but for a while she was so happy to be with Tom. And then she felt the tears on her face.

'You know, Tom, you really disappointed me,' she muttered. 'I thought that we were starting to…starting to mean something to each other. Perhaps I misread the signs. But after you kissed me on the hill, I—'

He came round to her side of the table, sat by her with his arm round her and gently kissed her. It was so good to lean against his chest, feel the warmth of his breath on her neck, the strength of his arm holding her. She could feel the beating of his heart, which seemed faster than it should have been.

'You mean a lot to me,' he murmured. 'An awful lot. I've never met a girl like you. But I can see what this place means to you—the country, your friends, your family. And in a year I'll be finished here. I'll be back in a hospital in some grimy bit of London. I'll be gone and you'll be here. This can only be a temporary thing and I don't want to hurt you.'

She pushed herself upright and stared into those gorgeous green eyes. 'I can tell there's something you're not saying,' she said. 'Something you're not telling me. You told me the truth, didn't you? You're not married or anything like that?'

He laughed and she could see the genuine amusement in his face. 'No, I'm not married,' he said. 'Not even engaged. And never have been.' He looked thoughtful for a moment. 'Well, actually I was engaged once. And I hoped to get married.'

'Engaged! Who to?'

'I asked my friend Lucy Halloran to marry me and she said yes. Mind you, we were both only seven at the time.'

'In that case I'll forgive you,' she said unable to hide a smile and laid her head on his chest again.

'I know I shouldn't have come here,' Tom said after a while, 'I have no right to, no right at all. But I just couldn't stay away.'

'Hush,' Nikki whispered. 'You know how welcome you are.'

In bed late that night Nikki remembered the sadness on Tom's face when he'd said he would be gone in a year. If it made him so sad, why did he have to go? Perhaps he was going to be a great orthopaedic surgeon. He was certainly a great GP. Who could tell which was the right career?

Then she thought some more. She realised that he hadn't answered her question. There *was* something that he was keeping from her. She wished she knew what it was.

The following Tuesday, by chance she met Meriel in town. They stopped to chat a while, and Meriel asked Nikki what was to happen to Toby.

'He's volunteered to go back into hospital,' Nikki said. 'Joe's arranged for him to try a new drug regime—perhaps they can get his behaviour under control again.'

'I hope so. I want to see him at the balls—but I don't want to see you lying on the floor again.' Nikki could tell that Meriel meant this, and she felt rather pleased.

They chatted inconsequentially for a couple of minutes and then Meriel said, with an air of great unconcern, 'Seen much of Tom Murray? I thought he might ring me, but he hasn't.'

'He's been very busy,' said Nikki, knowing this was true. 'Probably he just hasn't had time.'

'I guess so. It's not a great affair, of course, but I like him.'

'He's a nice guy,' said Nikki.

'If you're going to Leeds again tomorrow, could I have a lift?' Nikki asked Tom, 'that is, if it's not inconvenient or anything. I need to do a bit of shopping and I gather you're going down there again.'

It was the Thursday after the ball. She had come

back early to the surgery to try to catch him, not having seen him since the previous Saturday night.

Tom looked uncomfortable. 'I don't know,' he began. 'Do you think it's a good thing? I mean, we—'

'Look, don't be silly. I need a lift and a car to carry stuff back in. And I want to go fast in that red sports car of yours. We agreed that we're going to be friends. It makes perfect sense to go there together. Don't worry, I'll leave you to see your patient and not interfere, and I won't ask awkward or embarrassing questions.'

He smiled. 'That's not like you. But I can't imagine anyone I'd rather drive with. Early start, though. Set off at half past six?'

'I'm a country girl. That's late.'

When he'd gone she wished they didn't have to keep insisting that they were only friends. They were so much more than that. But if that's what he wanted to pretend—so be it.

There was little on the roads so early in the morning and they enjoyed the trip across the moors. Nikki tried to get him to talk about the patient he was going to visit in Leeds but he didn't seem to want to talk about him. 'I'd rather watch the scenery and have you tell me about growing up round here,' he said. 'We'll leave worrying about medicine till I get to the hospital.' So she talked about her early years and he seemed fascinated.

Eventually they reached the outskirts of Leeds. It was a city she'd visited often before, she quite liked it. But as they made their slow progress through the suburbs, she had to ask him. 'Do you really want to live in a city, Tom? Put up with this every day?'

'I now understand the attraction of living in the

country—I didn't before. But a big city has its good points, too. Now, where do you want to go shopping?'

He dropped her off at the shopping centre and they arranged to meet in the main foyer of the hospital at exactly four o'clock. They both knew the hospital, a vast place on the city outskirts, and he said she would be sure to miss him if she tried to get to the orthopaedic department. There was a café in the foyer so it would be easy to spot each other there.

Usually she enjoyed her trips to the city. There were the shops that held the things that Hambleton never saw, the cafés and restaurants that offered a far wider choice than was available to her at home. But today she was restless. The things that had to be bought she bought quickly. Then she found she had no interest in browsing the boutiques, looking at the latest fashions. She decided she'd go to the hospital early.

It was only half past one when her taxi pulled up outside the foyer. She took her parcels inside and when he'd seen her nurse's badge the porter agreed to store them till later. She had a sandwich and a coffee in the café and then decided to walk round the grounds. The hospital was extensive, set in a grassy, well-wooded area, with various departments scattered among the trees.

It was still a fine day, and she thought how much more pleasant walking here was than pounding along the city streets.

Then, by sheer chance, she saw Tom.

He was sitting at a table, his back to her, his head in his hands as if he were thinking something dispiriting. She started to walk up to him but hesitated.

She had never seen him with his head in his hands before. There was a tree to one side and she edged into its shade and stood there to watch him. She didn't intend to spy—she just thought this wasn't a good time to talk to him.

After a while she saw him look at his watch, rise wearily and walk to the nearest building. She followed him at a safe distance. Then she blinked. This was the entrance lobby to a department, but not Orthopaedics. It was marked ONCOLOGY. What was Tom doing in a cancer department?

She felt apprehensive. There must, of course, be some obvious explanation and she was probably just being silly, but she felt apprehensive.

She waited a while and then marched boldly into the entrance lobby. There was no sign of Tom so she went to the receptionist and said, 'I'm here to pick up Dr Murray. I think I'm a bit early—do you know when he'll be ready?'

'He's just gone in to see the consultant,' the young woman replied.

'So I am early, no matter. Could I ask how he is?' Somehow Nikki managed to keep her voice calm and controlled, though she could feel her heart beating like a hammer.

It wasn't the sort of question she should ask and it certainly wasn't the sort of question the receptionist should answer. Very properly, she didn't. 'You'll have to ask Dr Murray that. He should be about another half-hour.' But Nikki could tell by the tone of her voice and the lowered head that the news wasn't good.

She nodded, as if it were all one to her. 'I think I'll sit outside in the sun. Don't tell him I'm waiting, he'll only get anxious. Thanks for your help.' She somehow managed to smile and walked away.

There was a bench that faced the building entrance and she sat there. She tried to quell the turmoil of anxiety raging within her. There was no need to panic yet, not until she had all the facts. She was jumping to conclusions, they might all be entirely wrong. There were any number of simple explanations that would make all these worries instantly disappear, and she would laugh at her previous apprehension.

But all the time there was one horrific question in her mind. Had Tom got cancer? And if he had, where?

She knew, of course, that great steps had been taken in the treatment of cancer over the past twenty-five years. There had been no sudden leap forward but a steady increase in knowledge and treatment. Infant leukaemia, for example. Thirty years ago only one in every ten patients survived. Now perhaps only one in every ten patients died. But that was still too many!

Did Tom have cancer? As she thought things over, so much of his puzzling behaviour now made sense. And a new emotion slowly grew within her. She was desperately upset, of course, but now she was also angry.

Eventually she saw him come out of the entrance, turn and make his way towards the main foyer. He didn't see her. She stood, ran across the grass to meet him.

He looked confused when she appeared in front of him. 'Nikki! You're early, we're not due to meet for another couple of hours.'

'I got tired of shopping. I didn't expect to see you coming out of the oncology department, Tom.'

'Just dropped in to see an old acquaintance,' he mumbled, not meeting her eyes. 'We were at medical school together and...' Then he looked at her face and decided not to say any more.

'You're hiding things from me that I should know,' Nikki said bitterly. 'Whatever we are to each other, I'm entitled to know. We should share the bad things as well as the good.'

Tom nodded slowly.

'Please. Come here and sit on the bench and tell me about it. And don't pretend and don't lie because I don't think I could cope with it. I don't know whether to be really angry with you or to cry.'

She felt her voice quaver.

He put his arms round her shoulders, gave her a friendly hug. 'Things aren't all that bad, Nikki,' he said.

'I said no more lying!'

He was silent for a moment. 'Well, things could be better,' he said.

They sat side by side on the bench. It was still a beautiful afternoon, the trees and the lawns stretched out in front of them. The occasional patient wandered by, and a couple of nurses walking in the fast way they always had. There was even a bird singing in the tree behind them. And it all seemed unreal to Nikki. This peace wasn't the truth, it was a lie.

She looked at the man by her side, his tie loosened, his jacket slung over his shoulder. Now she knew, she could understand the thinness of his face, the pain lines round his mouth and eyes.

'We'll start again,' she said quietly, 'and you can tell me everything. Joe knows, doesn't he?'

Tom nodded. 'It wouldn't have been fair to come to work for him and not tell him. I had both chemotherapy and radiotherapy before I took the job. I'm in remission now. I need to come down to see a consultant every month or so and we cooked up the story about me having to see a patient here. But I can still be an ordinary doctor.'

'You're not an ordinary doctor! You're a good doctor!' Nikki knew her voice was shrill but there was nothing she could do about it. 'Tom, please. Start at the beginning and tell me all about it.'

He didn't look at her but fixed his eyes in the middle distance. When he started to speak his voice was harsh. With a great pang of pity she realised how hard this was for him. But she had to know!

'Anyone can get ill,' he said, 'even doctors. It can strike just like that—with no cause, no reason. I suppose we ought to be able to expect it, but that's difficult. Medics think that other people get ill—not themselves.

'I was working hard, studying like mad, making my way up the ladder. I had no time for anything but orthopaedics. And I loved it. Then I started to feel tired. I thought at first that it was just a case of burn-out, that I had been overdoing things, and I could work through it. Then I got even more tired. I started losing weight and sometimes at night I woke up drenched with sweat.'

He smiled wearily. 'Perhaps I thought that if I ignored it, it would go away. I was a doctor, not a patient! And, then quite by chance, one night I felt my neck—and there was a lump on the lymph gland.

So I thought—just for a laugh, you know—I'd have myself looked at.

'I thought just a quick examination. No chance! I had a biopsy, X-rays, a CT scan. I was referred ever upwards, from the A and E doctor to the consultant. And eventually it was diagnosed that I had Hodgkin's disease. Cancer of the lymph glands. Stage Three B.'

'I've heard of it,' Nikki said, 'though I've never nursed it. Don't most people recover?'

'Most do. A few don't—though we doctors still don't know why. The chances normally aren't too bad. With Hodgkin's disease there's a final success rate of about two in three, perhaps the odds are even better. At present I don't feel too bad. I come here for a regular check-up and so far things have been fine. But there's that ultimate uncertainty. You never really know.'

She could hardly bear the starkness of his words.

'So what made you come up to Hambleton?'

'The prospect of possible death fixes the mind,' he said cheerfully. 'It made me look at what I had, decide what I wanted to do. I thought I needed a change. I loved orthopaedics, but there was little point in training for a career that I might not have. I wanted to live a little. I saw the advert for the job at Hambleton and thought it would be a good place to live a totally different life. It might be a short life but I was determined to have a good one.'

'That's why you fell on my roof,' she said slowly. 'That's why you wanted to look at the chicks.'

'True. Something I'd never done or seen before. Now was the time—before the possibility of it being too late.'

There was so much to take in, so much to think about. Now so many of Tom's previously puzzling actions made sense. 'You kept away from me…tried not to fall in love with me…said you only wanted to be friends…because…'

'Because I didn't want you to be hurt,' he said. 'There was no way I wanted you to be in love with a man who could die.'

Then his voice changed from sympathy to harshness. 'And there's more. I told you my mother died when I was eight. Well, she died of Hodgkin's disease. I know it can't be inherited, I know you can't tell the progress of a disease. But I watched her die when I was eight. It was painful—for her and me. And I'm not going to have anyone I love suffer from that uncertainty.'

He laughed, and Nikki wondered how he could. 'I've never felt the way about any woman the way I feel about you, Nikki. I think…well, I think I could love you. It would be so much easier if I didn't. Because I'm not going to put anyone I love through what I went through.'

Nikki could hardly cope with this. She was a nurse, had nursed people she'd known would die. She'd seen her grandfather die and it had been a calm and proper end after a long and happy life. He'd accepted his death willingly, and after weeping she had accepted it too. But this was different! It was much harder to cope with the threatened death of someone so young, so full of promise. She had to think it now—it was the threatened death of someone she loved! No, she couldn't cope. So she burst into tears.

Tom put his arm round her, pulled her to him and

waited till the torrents of sobbing had slowed. Then he offered her his handkerchief. 'Come on, Nikki, it's not so bad,' he said gently. 'I can deal with it.'

'*You* can deal with it! Tom, it's far, far better to share problems. I want to be with you, to help you. Now, no more rubbish about us only being friends. We're more than that! I want you to admit it. Please?'

He smiled. 'We're more than friends, Nikki. And it makes me feel so good to say it.'

'So we're going to share. We can work this out together.'

Tom's smile swiftly changed into a frown. 'I didn't want this. I wanted to keep things from you. Now you know why I didn't want you to get too fond of me. Can't you see there's no future in it for you?'

This made her angry. 'Fond of you! Who's fond of you? What we're talking about is love. And it can't be switched on and off like a light. It just is. And my feelings aren't for you to decide, I decide them myself.'

'But I don't want to hurt you! You're not going to sit by and wonder all your life just how well I am.'

'That's for me to decide, Tom.'

They sat in silence for a while, and then Nikki said, 'There is one thing you can do for me.'

'And that is?'

'Tell Meriel McCarthy that there's no hope for her.'

CHAPTER SIX

THE trip back was calmer. After a bright day they were blessed with a lovely evening, it seemed to soothe both of them. When Tom could, he drove holding Nikki's hand. It was a tiny intimacy but it meant a lot to her.

They didn't talk much. There was a feeling that quite enough had been said. Neither wanted any more emotion for a while. But they were easier with each other now that things had been aired. Nikki didn't feel Tom's actions were inexplicable any more. Now she knew what the problem was, she could try to deal with it.

'Emotion is tiring,' he said after a while. 'It also makes you hungry. Would you like to stop at one of these country pubs, have a meal?'

Now he'd mentioned it, she realised she was hungry. But going to a pub or restaurant was the last thing she wanted. 'I don't really fancy a public place,' she said. 'I don't want to be surrounded by people. If you can hold out, will you come back and have a meal with me? I've nothing much in, but I can do you something. Or we can fetch a take-away.'

'I'll be happy with anything so long as it's with you.'

So they waited till they got home, then she prepared a simple meal and he fetched a bottle of wine. They ate outside. Afterwards they sat in the lengthening shadows as the sun went down.

By mutual silent agreement they said nothing about what had been disclosed. That would come later. And as Nikki sat there she came to a conclusion.

'We just can't talk any more,' she said. 'There's too much to think about. But we now know it can't be over between us, we've got some kind of a future. So we should do something. This weekend is out, I'm expected at my parents' farm. So…if not before, then next Wednesday night. That's in five days, it'll give me a chance to…to think about things. We get together and we talk.'

'You already know what I'm going to say.'

'It's old men who get set in their ways and views—you're still young. Doctors deal with people and they have to be flexible with them. You're going to be flexible with me and yourself. That's all I ask.'

He seemed to consider. 'All right, then. But I'll kiss you and then we'll both go to bed. We're both tired, we need time.'

So he came to kiss her. 'You know, I'm glad you found out I was ill,' he said quietly. 'I didn't like hiding things from you. And now, somehow, I feel better. I'm sharing.' Then he walked across to the White House.

Nikki got into bed with mixed emotions. Now she knew what he felt for her, and that made her happy. There was still the horror at learning of his disease, but with the horror came determination. She now knew what they were fighting and together they could fight it. He had better not think that everything had already been decided and he was going it alone.

Brassenthwaite was a tiny village. Originally it had been much larger, built for the workers of a now abandoned quarry some half a mile away. There was a church and a church hall, but very little else. The mobile library called, the mobile shop called, there was a bus three times a day. If you went shopping by bus you had to time your visits carefully. And there was a school bus, a small one. But often in winter the steep road up to Brassenthwaite was closed.

But some people liked the village. There were the views, and many valued the solitude. Nikki always enjoyed her visits there.

She was calling on Ms Pink—never Miss or Mrs. 'I'll specify my marital status when men do the same,' Nikki had been told. 'And not until then. But I'd like you to call me Penny. Penny Pink—quite a name, isn't it?'

'Quite a name—and I think it suits you,' Nikki had said.

Penny was a woman of about forty, with long hair, long skirts, sandals but never tights. Her face was handsome, striking rather than beautiful. Nikki got on well with her. Penny was different—but she didn't force her difference on you.

She had bought an end-of-terrace stone cottage and it was a comfortable if unusual home. Penny lived with her nine-year-old son, Jake, apparently a computer whiz, whose time at the screen had to be limited. Most of the time they spent happily together in the kitchen.

The front room had been turned into a workshop, with a small furnace, welding equipment, saws, drills and a tiny lathe. Penny made jewellery—beautiful but often barbaric in design. Unlike many of the craftsmen who had come up to the moors, she didn't sell her goods herself. They were sent to London. 'I didn't come to this beautiful place to be a shop-keeper, Nikki.'

Penny was a diabetic. Nikki dropped in about once every three weeks to make sure that Penny's medication was in order and that all was going well.

'What about this new technique of planting a capsule of insulin under the skin?' Penny asked as they shared a cup of coffee. 'It releases itself gradually—it would mean that I didn't have to stick needles into myself every day.'

'I've heard of it,' Nikki said cautiously, 'but it's not yet on general release. Carry on with the injections for now and we can update you with any further details we get.'

She liked talking to Penny, who was intelligent about her medication. They chatted about life in general and then they heard the sound of a small disturbance outside, the muttering of young voices, followed by a muted sobbing. Penny opened the door and there stood a young lad of about ten, obviously deciding to get his defence in first. 'We told him not to go through the fence, Ms Pink, but he just did. And then he fell a bit.'

He moved to one side and another young lad escorted Jake in. Jake was white-faced, shaking, clutching a blood-stained and grubby handkerchief to his arm.

'You've been to the quarry, haven't you?' his mother said reprovingly. 'You know I've told you to keep away. Now no computer for a week.'

'Oh, Mum!'

'I mean it. Teach you to do as you're told.'

Penny turned to the other two downcast lads. 'And, you two, you know it's dangerous out there. Tell your mothers what's happened—or I will.'

From the guilty faces Nikki gathered that the two had been warned before. 'Here you are.' Penny gave them each a large wholemeal biscuit from a barrel. 'Now, off you go—I don't think Jake will be out for a while.'

Nikki sat Jake in an easy chair, reaching for a coat to put round him. He might be a little shocked. 'Could you make him a warm drink, Penny? Cocoa or something like that would be fine. And very sweet.' Gently she prised away Jake's fingers.

It was a nasty gash, just above the elbow. There were flakes of rust there and it would need suturing after being cleaned. From her bag Nikki took a sterile pad and told Jake to hold it to the wound. 'How did you fall, Jake? Did you hurt yourself anywhere else?'

'I only hurt my arm—and my chest a bit.'

'We'll have a look.' When she had worked in A and E it had been drilled into her not just to treat the injury presented but to check everywhere. Patients often didn't realise they'd been hurt in more than one place. So Nikki opened Jake's shirt and examined his chest. There would be a small bruise, she decided, but she didn't think any bones were broken. The rest of his body she would check later.

Penny knew what to do. She fetched a bowl of warm water and then put her arm round her son to comfort him. 'I did warn you about the quarry,' she said. 'I knew something like this would happen. But perhaps I'll change my mind about the computer time. Perhaps.'

The cut wasn't too bad. Nikki washed and dressed

it then decided to manage with three butterfly stitches. She asked if Penny was certain that Jake was up to date with his tetanus jabs. He was. Lastly Nikki asked him to move his fingers. There seemed to be some lack of movement. When she got him to squeeze her hand she could hardly feel it.

'What did your arm feel like when you fell, Jake?'

'Well, I fell on my funny bone. It went all pins and needlesy. It still feels a bit queer.'

Nikki pondered. It was almost certainly nothing but a nerve could have been severed. This was out of her league. She could arrange for Jake to be sent to A and E, but that would be a major expedition. However, she did know a doctor.

She knew Tom would be on his rounds. He had arranged with Joe that he would do most of the out-of-surgery calls. That suited both of them. So Nikki went outside and called Tom on his mobile, hoping that he wasn't behind some great hill that would blank the signal.

This was business, of course, but still her fingers trembled slightly when she jabbed at the numbers. She hadn't seen him for five days—they had kept apart after her discovery in Leeds. They'd needed time to think.

'Tom? Where are you and are you busy?'

'I'm not busy. I'm on my way back now from Kellett. I've just seen Mrs Farmiloe. It was a false alarm, by the way, she didn't have a heart attack.'

'It was indigestion,' Nikki said.

'It was indeed. I wish I could diagnose by remote control as well as you can.'

That morning Nikki had seen a list of Tom's calls. By the side of Mrs Farmiloe's name she had pencilled the query, 'Indigestion?' 'I've known Mrs Farmiloe for a few years. You'd be surprised at the number of illnesses she's suspected which have come down to indigestion.'

'Indigestion being a posh word for over-eating,' he said heavily. 'Now, it's lovely to chat, but is this a professional call?'

'Professional, I'm afraid. I've got this young lad…' She described Jake's symptoms.

'I think you're right, it's probably nothing. But I'd like to have a look. Where are you?'

'Brassenthwaite. It's about eleven miles by the main road but only seven if you come direct. Have you got your map there?' She had advised him to buy a large-scale map of the area. Many of the places they visited were only marked on a larger map.

She heard a rustling sound. 'I've found Brassenthwaite.'

'Good.' She knew this district backwards—which was the best way to bring him? 'Come off the main road two miles out of Kellett and left onto a really small road….got it? Now down to where it's marked as an ex-army camp. You can cut through there to the other side of the stream where there's a B road. That leads eventually to Brassenthwaite.'

'It all seems clear. I'm on my way.'

'I'll be waiting for you. The last cottage on the right on the main road.'

Nikki went back into the house to speak to Penny. 'The doctor's on the way but there's no need to worry. Just have Jake sit here quietly.'

'I could go to my room, Mum,' a weak voice suggested.

'Near your computer? No chance. Just lie there.'

Penny made them both another coffee and then said, rather shyly, 'Would you like to come and see what I'm doing now? I've been given a commission and I've made a few drawings.'

Nikki looked at pictures of rings. They were all fine pieces but... 'I like that one best.' She pointed to a green stone in a swirly gold setting.

'So do I,' said a gratified Penny, 'but my client asked for this one.'

Nikki peered at the alternative. 'It's lovely,' she said. 'It's really lovely. But that one is the best—and it's glorious.'

Five minutes later her mobile rang again.

'Fine through the army camp,' Tom's voice said, 'but you didn't tell me that I should be driving a tank.'

'A tank? What are you talking about?'

'I followed your instructions, they were perfect. But there's been some heavy traffic through here and it's cut up the banks of the stream, so the path is a sea of mud and I'm stuck in the middle of it. Not a happy chap, Nikki. I've got a high-powered red sports car and it's covered with mud and won't move. I'd be better off with a tractor. You've got the local knowledge—which garage shall I call?'

'Just wait there. I'm on my way.'

She had grown up on the farm, driving her father's tractor. At nine she'd had her first lesson driving the diesel Land Rover round the fields. She was happy with four-wheel-drive vehicles and could negotiate any terrain. When she'd got the job of District Nurse she'd known she'd have to get to difficult addresses so she'd bought herself a tough vehicle that would go anywhere. Not like a smart red sports car.

She explained what had happened to Penny, who laughed. Nikki set off, and twenty minutes later she saw Tom. By now he knew enough to always carry boots with him and was standing there in wellingtons and his smart doctor's suit. The red car that had driven so fast to and from Leeds now looked out of place in a sea of mud. She hadn't realised just how deep it was, and felt rather guilty.

Nikki put on her own boots and took out the tow rope that she always carried. 'I'm sorry,' she said, 'I should have realised that it could be this bad. And look at your car!'

He shrugged. 'I've more important things to worry about. These things happen.'

She liked the way he never got angry, liked his constant calmness. But sometimes she wondered what there might be bubbling underneath that easy-going exterior. Was he raging there?

'We don't need a garage, I'll pull you out myself,' she said.

'Can you do it?' He looked surprised.

'That's what four-wheel-drive vehicles are for. We'll soon shift that little red thing.' Carrying the rope, she gingerly stepped into the mud.

'Here, let me do that. You wait by the car and—'

'No. This is my job. I got you into this and I'm used to this kind of thing and— Oh!'

She *was* used to conditions like this, sometimes she thought she'd been born wearing a pair of wellingtons. But she slipped and fell anyway. Her foot turned on a stone hidden in the mud and she fell backwards, sitting down in the mud. It was sticky and wet and cold and she felt an absolute fool.

'I can see that you're used to this kind of thing,'

Tom said urbanely, trying to hide his laughter. 'Here, let me help you up.'

He offered her his hands and for a moment she was tempted to sit there and pull him down into the mud next to her. He guessed her thoughts. 'You do,' he whispered, 'and I'll not be responsible for the consequences.' It was both threat and promise. So she let him heave her upright.

It wasn't a romantic moment. They were standing in a pool of mud and she was wet, cold and uncomfortable. But he didn't let go of her hands and they stood silently facing each other. He kissed her, a soft, gentle kiss, with only their hands and their lips touching. Her eyes closed and she wondered what might be, what could be. Then she stopped thinking and realised how foolishly happy she was, just being there with him. After an eternity their kiss ended, but he still held her hands. In his face she could see mirrored all the emotions she felt and wondered if they had ever been as close as they were right now. But the moment had to pass. They were professional people and had work to do.

'Go and try to scrape some of that mud off and I'll attach this,' he said, taking the rope from her.

'Tom?' When he looked at her she wiped a finger on her muddy skirt, then gently rubbed it down his nose. He stood still, letting her. 'Now we're a bit more equal,' she said.

Two minutes later the rope was stretched between the two cars. Nikki kicked off her boots, got into her car and waved to him. This was something she had done many times before. Gently, she let the clutch in. The rope tightened, strained and then with a squelching noise Tom's car lurched out of the mud.

She pulled it until it was on the firmness of the secondary road, then stopped to untie the rope.

'I see you've wiped the mud off your face,' she said.

'I see you've not got all the mud off your uniform,' he replied with a grin. 'But lead on and we'll go to see Jake.' She turned to get in her car but before she could do so he quickly kissed her. 'I could get to like this,' he said.

Penny lent Nikki a towel and the use of the bathroom while Tom examined Jake. She saw him making Jake bend his hand, running his fingers up and down his arm. Then she went to the bathroom. Sending for Tom had been the right thing to do.

When she came down she found him drinking more coffee with Penny and looking at her sketches of rings. Addressing both Nikki and Penny, he explained the situation. 'It was a deep cut, either the medial or the radial nerve could have been damaged. But I think he's all right. However, if he doesn't have the full use of his hand tomorrow, then please ring me.'

'OK,' said Penny, 'I will. And if you're in the area, you know you can always drop in—you and Nikki, that is.' She looked at Tom approvingly, and Nikki could see his charm had worked on Penny.

All three of them looked at the sketches of the rings for a moment, and Tom agreed that the one with the green stone was by far the most attractive. But time was passing. They had to leave.

Outside he stopped her. 'I suppose we'd both better get our cars cleaned up,' he said, 'get rid of some of this mud. Nikki, where would be the best place to get rid of this red monster and buy something a bit more suitable? I want a four-wheel-drive like yours.'

She was flattered that he should ask her. 'Ken Handy, a friend of mine just out of town, will find you something,' she said. 'He'll give you a good price, because he likes doctors. Last year we looked after his son, who had an accident in the yard. But are you sure you want to change? If you leave here in a year's time, you might want a sports car and—'

'I'm not thinking much beyond the end of this year,' he said. 'I'm not making any plans. It's great when you decide not to worry about what might happen.'

It shocked her as she realised what he meant and her dismay must have shown on her face. 'Just my way of handling things,' he said softly. 'If you accept that things could be bad you can only be surprised when things turn out for the better. And so far my life is turning out for the better. I feel good about it. Don't let me get you down.'

But it was a while before she could say, 'If you want to see Ken Handy, I'll go with you this evening.'

'Fine. Will you ring him now and explain what I want?'

'Are you sure you're not moving too fast, Tom?'

'It's the way I like to do things now. The way I need to do things.' There was that determined cheerfulness again.

So she rang Ken and arranged that Tom would call to see him that evening.

'You will come with me?' Tom asked, 'I like doing things with you.'

'I'll come with you. I like your company, too. In

fact, I more than like it. Being with you is...' Her voice faltered.

'Is as good for you as it is for me. Nikki, that is wonderful.'

What to wear? She found herself wondering this more and more when she went out with Tom. What she wanted was something that would be right, but that would impress. Well, that was every girl's idea.

Eventually she decided on trousers. She'd be walking round workshops, perhaps climbing in and out of cars. But they were black satin trousers. And the blouse on top was of white silk. She had to change her bra, of course—not the serviceable one she wore with her uniform, but something more dainty and lacy.

Tom was in his favourite black again, now dark jeans and a thin woollen sweater. He had cleaned the mud from the inside of his car and had had the outside washed at a garage.

As they drove slowly down the Hambleton high street Nikki felt half excited, half nervous. She wasn't sure why. She thought that this evening would turn into something more than an expedition to buy a car. Then she realised she'd decided that it was going to be something more. Things between her and Tom were different now.

But first, the car. Ken was waiting for them, wearing his usual shapeless set of overalls. She had rarely seen him in anything else. Ken would rather mend cars than sell them—but he did both. Introductions were made, followed by the usual couple of minutes of gossip. Then Ken went to look at Tom's car while Tom inspected the stock of four-wheel-drives.

'What kind of car do you want?' she asked.

'I'm not sure. But I'm tired of red. It'll have to be a blue one, I think.'

She punched his arm. 'Don't joke. Buying a car is a serious business. You ought to hear my dad when he's getting a new tractor.'

Ken rejoined them and they quickly narrowed the field down to two. Then Tom picked a diesel four-wheel-drive that was tough enough to go anywhere on the moors but still smart enough to drive through town. The paperwork hardly took any time, then they were driving out in a new vehicle.

Nikki was amazed. 'I've never bought anything that fast in my life! I spend more time choosing a lipstick than you did a car.'

'I like to get things settled. And Ken says I can take it back any time in the next fortnight if I'm not happy with it. But I will be. Now, I want to play with my new toy. Shall we go on a drive together?'

'I'd very much like that.' Tom looked at her and knew what she wanted. 'Afterwards we could go back to your place and talk. If that's OK with you, Nikki?'

'That would be good.' She smiled.

'Well, then, let's drive up onto a peak.'

For a while they drove along the local narrow roads, and then she took him to some abandoned mineworkings where he could practise some off-road driving. He was a quick study. 'No more getting stuck in the mud,' he said.

'Don't rely on that. Even this warhorse could need pulling out some time.'

He glanced at his watch. 'I'm ravenous. You've been good to me, showing me all this, so I'll take you to dinner to thank you. What's that pub like that we just passed? Good food?'

'I've heard it's fantastic. And there's a great view out at the back.'

So they went to the Cross Foxes, a grey stone building that had been converted into an inn two hundred years previously. They sat out at the back in a conservatory overlooking a deep valley. The food might have been fantastic, but afterwards Nikki couldn't remember anything about it. She knew she enjoyed it—but she enjoyed Tom's company more.

They talked about her early life, her ambitions. 'I couldn't make up my mind whether to be a farmer or a nurse. I had one of each as a parent—and each recommended that I should follow the other's job. Very confusing for a young girl.'

He grinned. 'It would have served them both right if you had done something totally different. Become a model or an actress.'

'Model or actress? Never, they're just not me. I've got to be organising people. Can't you tell that I'm bossy?'

'You're not bossy, you're just concerned for people. And you have the face and the figure of a model or actress,' he said softly. 'You're certainly slim enough. But you smile more than the average model, and that's rather nice.'

'Hmm,' she said, blushing slightly. 'Did you meet many models in London? I know you met at least one actress.'

'I used to go to a pub in north London where TV actors and models were sometimes seen. The landlord specialised in beer—you get a lot of beer fanatics there. And then this model—she's quite well known, but I won't tell you her name—anyway, she would come in and ask for a glass of water. But no lemon. Calories in fruit, you know.'

She giggled. 'That's an exaggeration!'

'Only a small one. But that's enough of talking about thin people. Makes me feel embarrassed.'

'You're hardly fat.'

'Result of the treatment I had. A side effect is weight loss.'

'Does it feel good to enjoy yourself and forget for a while?' she asked softly.

He looked into her eyes. 'Unbelievably good. Now, tell me what sort of sheep those are. If I'm to talk to the local farmers I have to be able to carry on an intelligent conversation.'

'As a conversation change that was less than subtle,' she said, 'so in revenge I'll tell you all I know about sheep. And it's your bad luck that I know rather a lot. I'm going to bore you sheepish.'

'I could never be bored, listening to you.' He smiled. 'It's getting late. Shall I ask for the bill?'

'Yes, please. Now we've got some talking to do.'

The evening was still warm. They climbed into his new vehicle and he kissed her as she sat beside him. But her mood had changed. She'd had a wonderful evening but this was the time to be serious. Things had to be sorted out.

'Shall we go to the White House or your caravan for this talk?' he asked.

'The caravan, I think. I've bought a bottle of wine specially for the occasion.' Then she realised the trap she was falling into. There was a danger that he would try to avoid a real confrontation by joking about things, refusing to take them seriously. She was determined she wasn't going to have that.

'You're not to make fun of me or of us,' she said. 'That's an escape and an evasion.'

'Possibly. Sometimes I find it a way of coping with things.'

He had to slow down as ahead of them was a set of men in filthy overalls, carrying great coils of rope and with helmets on their heads. 'Cavers,' she said. 'There's the entrance to an old mine just down there.' She shivered. 'The very idea gets me scared.'

Then she decided it was time to be bold. 'Are you scared, Tom? You don't seem to be. Or do you just bottle it up, keep it to yourself?'

He drove so long without replying that she thought he wasn't going to. But then he said, 'I used to be scared. I used to think that it was all most unfair. At one stage I was terrified. I'd wake up in the middle of the night thinking that perhaps I was going to die and that would be terrible. But not now.'

He stretched his arm out, ruffled her hair. 'You should know that talking about fear makes you afraid, Nikki. I want to wait till we get back.'

'All right,' she said in a small voice. 'Anyway, we're nearly there.'

It was still warm enough to sit out on the patio. Nikki fetched the bottle of wine and poured out two glasses. 'Help me to understand, Tom. Please, tell me how you used to be scared and why you're not now,' she requested. She didn't want to, but she needed to start this conversation at once.

He sipped his wine, staring out into the distance. 'I used to think that being afraid of something that might happen was self-defeating,' he said. 'It was better to be resigned. So I expected death, and that was calming.' He shrugged at her fierce expression.

'Sounds like giving up to me. It's the old question. If you drink half a glass of water, is the glass now half full or half empty? If you think the glass is half full then that's life-enhancing.'

He laughed. 'I can always trust you not to let me get away with anything, Nikki. That's why I...I...'

'You'll have to say it now.'

'All right. That's why I love you. I think.'

'"I think." Trust a man to leave himself a way out.' She sipped her wine and then went on, 'So what do you feel about being ill now? And why have you changed?'

'Meeting you has changed me. You've made me realise that life has so much more to offer than I thought, so I'm going to take what I can and you can help me. Today, for example—just ordinary things but it has been so good because I've done them with you.' Then his face darkened. 'But I'm still determined that I won't hurt you.'

'I'll worry about the hurt. I'm going to shock you into realising I'm right.'

She had been thinking about this all week. Now she knew she was going to gamble—but what she intended to say felt so right. She knew she had just been hard on Tom, and it hurt her. She had spent hours trying to imagine what he must be suffering, he didn't need her to make things worse. But perhaps this would work.

'I love you,' she said. 'You may be ill, not sure what might happen, but I love you. I've had boy-friends before but so far I've never...you know.' She took a deep breath and looked into his eyes. 'Tom, I want you to stay the night. Come to bed with me.'

'But, Nikki!' he protested, 'I've told you, my future is doubtful and I—'

'We've talked about that, Tom. You can't go on thinking that way all the time.'

He shook his head. 'I know, Nikki. You're right. I want you so much. But are you sure you're not doing this because I—?'

'Don't even say it,' she said quietly. 'I'm a nurse, I don't sleep with people because I pity them. I want to do it because I love you, Tom. Can't you see that?'

'Yes. I can see it.' For a while he looked at her, his expression unreadable. Then he stood and came round the table. He took her hands in his, drew her to her feet, then kissed her. She felt apprehensive at first but then she knew that everything would be all right. He put his arm round her waist and led her into the caravan.

It was a double bed—just—but in a tiny bedroom. Nikki had drawn the curtains and switched on the bedhead lights, so that the room was dimly lit. There were her built-in wardrobes, chests of drawers, a little dressing-table. Pictures of her family fastened to the walls. Her lightweight summer quilt with its pretty floral pattern. All so familiar, so comforting. But now appearing strangely new.

Nikki was nervous. She had made the offer but that had taken so much out of her that she now felt, well, uncertain. Perhaps a bit frightened. It was something that she longed to do so much, but she wasn't sure what to do next.

Tom seemed to realise how she felt. They sat side

by side on the bed to kick off their shoes. Then he
swiftly moved to the top of the bed and pulled her
back towards him so she was lying along his body,
her head under his chin. His arms were wrapped
loosely round her from behind and she lay there,
stroking his hands. It was a comfortable position, it
relaxed her.

Once again she looked round her room, gaining
strength from its sheer familiarity. But there was
something about it that was different, she felt different. Never had she lain on this bed with a man.

On her back she could feel the rise and fall of his
chest, the warmth of his body. There were the muscles of his thighs squeezing her gently. It was so
good to lie there.

He kissed the top of her head then bent down to
kiss her cheek—it was all he could reach. For the
moment that would do. But she could feel something
pulsing deep and slow inside her, an urgency that
was growing.

She was wearing a blouse that buttoned down the
front. After a while she unbuttoned it, managed to
wriggle out of it. Then she leaned forward and undid
her bra. She took his hands, rested them on her
breasts. And inside her, the pulsing quickened.

Her skin felt charged, electric. For a while he just
held her there, but then he stroked her and she felt
the peaks of her breasts come erect, and when he
touched them a soft moan escaped her. She hadn't
thought that such a simple caress could evoke so
much pleasure.

There was no need to hurry. His fingertips traced
lines along her naked body, sometimes grazing the
underneath of her arms, sometimes the curve of her

neck. Then they returned to her breasts. Her heart was beating faster now and her breathing deepened.

Neither of them felt the need to talk. Perhaps there had been too much covered up by speech, this was more honest.

She realised that his breathing was deeper too, she felt his chest rising more quickly under her. And as she stirred in pleasure she felt another, more obvious sign of his need for her.

In time, when they both were ready, he turned her round so they were facing each other. Now her arms were able to circle him and the kiss that followed seemed to stretch on into infinity. After a moment she eased him from her and helped him take off his shirt. The roughness of his skin against her breasts was almost more exciting than she could bear.

Another kiss, and then she fumbled at his belt. He leaned away from her, swept off his trousers in one swift movement. Then he did the same to her. Soon they were both naked.

She would not have thought it but, feeling the passion of his gaze, she revelled in letting him see all of her. She loved him, all this was hers to offer and she would offer it willingly. She wanted him desperately.

He kissed her again. Once more it felt so different when they were naked. She was conscious of her entire body—legs, thighs, hips, breasts, arms—pressed against his. It was if they had been made to fit together, there was no part of him she could not feel.

For moments they were crushed together. Then she found herself lying on her back, his body nearly on top of hers. It was what she needed, what they were inevitably moving towards. But first...

'In my bag,' she muttered, 'it's in the wardrobe, you must get my nurse's bag.'

He looked at her, puzzled. 'Your bag, sweetheart? What do you want?'

'Part of my job as a district nurse. Sometimes I give talks on contraception—there are things in my bag. Samples.'

'Oh, Lord, yes. Sweetheart, I had forgotten.'

She closed her eyes and lay there supremely content, knowing that the tiny last of her worries had been removed. There was the click of her bag opening, the rustle of paper. Then he came back to her.

She opened her arms to him, opened her body, too. It was magic. There was a moment of discomfort, a moment only of disbelief. But then it felt so easy. There was this sense of togetherness that drove them together to a swift and joint climax that was the most earth-shattering feeling she had ever experienced. She was lost in him, and then she wept through sheer happiness.

'You won't go,' she begged. 'You'll stay with me.'

'I'll stay with you as long as I can,' he whispered. Then they slept.

Nikki knew they both had to work the next morning. She woke early, clear-minded and happy, having slept better than she had done in weeks. Creeping out of the bedroom, she went to the kitchen to make them both tea.

Tom was awake when she returned and smiled at her sleepily. 'I cannot tell a lie,' he said. 'I heard the tinkle of cups. But I decided to stay here until called. I thought we might—'

'Drink tea,' she laughed, fending off his hands.

But when they had drunk the tea there was still time, and they made love again. It was just as wonderful when they could do it slowly and languorously. Then they lay there and looked at each other.

'Things have changed,' Tom said. 'How things have changed.'

'We're a couple and we're in love. You can't get rid of me now.' It wasn't a challenge, just a simple acceptance of a fact that both of them recognised.

'No, I can't get rid of you now. And, Lord knows, I don't want to… But, Nikki, I won't make you suffer, so I've got a suggestion. For the next three months let's just carry on as if everything were normal. Go out together as if we were an ordinary couple. We need to get to know each other, I need to meet your friends and family. Who knows? After a while it might be that you think I'm not the kind of man you want.'

'Possible,' she agreed, 'but I think most unlikely. I've never met anyone like you.' She thought about what he'd suggested. 'All right, if you want, for three months we carry on as if nothing was the matter. But, Tom, I love you, and people who are in love share things. If you get ill, I want you to be able to talk to me, to be able to—'

He leaned over to kiss her. 'I love you. And for three months we forget things and just go out together. Nikki, that will make me so happy, even though I wonder if it's really fair to you.'

'It's fair, it's what I want. But don't think that after three months I'm just going to give you up. I've got you now, Tom Murray, and I'm keeping you. Now, I suppose we ought to get dressed and go to work.'

'We'd better, yes. I must go home and change.' He kissed her again. 'I wonder what all my patients will think when they see my big smile.'

'I'll tell you tonight. My patients will see the same thing.'

That day was another of the summer days that made her happy to be alive—green fields, blue skies, the breeze like champagne. She called on George and Mary Dunmore, and thought that Mary was perhaps looking a bit better. She called on a young lad at a neighbouring farm who had gashed his thigh, changed his dressing and sternly told him that he was *not* to try to help in the fields. Then, since she was in the area, she went to call on her parents.

They were in together. She sat with them in the kitchen and drank tea. 'You've got a sparkle in your eye,' said her father with a smile. 'Any special reason?'

Was it that obvious? She thought of last night and this morning, then blushed and decided not to be too exact. 'I've been seeing quite a bit of Tom Murray,' she admitted. 'I...quite like him and I think he likes me. But it's early days yet.'

'He seemed a sound fellow,' her father said. 'A sensible man. I liked him, too.'

This was praise indeed from her father. 'Did you like him, Christine?' he asked. 'I know you didn't see much of him but did you like what you saw?'

Her mother paused before answering and Nikki looked at her curiously. Usually her parents agreed on almost everything. 'Didn't you like him, Mum?' she asked.

Her mother looked a little upset. 'Has he told you what's wrong with him?' she asked bluntly.

'Why should there be anything wrong with him?' Nikki knew her voice was faltering, but she couldn't change it.

'You're not the only medical person in the family,' her mother returned. 'Remember, I was a nurse for fifteen years. And there's something about that young man. He's ill, isn't he? Or he's recently been very ill.'

Nikki had forgotten how shrewd her mother was. But now she couldn't lie. 'He's got Hodgkin's disease,' she said. 'He's in remission now.'

Her mother knew at once, her father looked blank. 'It's a cancer,' her mother explained, 'a cancer of the lymphatic glands.'

'Can it be cured?' was his next question.

Her mother looked at Nikki, it was for her to answer. 'Probably not,' she said. 'Though many people live with it for years and their eventual cause of death is entirely something else.' She paused and then went on, 'He's all right for now, he's in remission, but he didn't want people to know about it. He kept it from me at first. He said he didn't want us getting too keen on each other because he's not too sure of his future. He said he didn't want me to suffer either.'

'It sounds like he cares about you very much,' said her father quietly, 'and I respect him for it.'

Her mother smiled. 'Can you bring him to tea, Nikki? On Sunday perhaps?'

'I'll certainly ask him. Don't forget, we're a big and frightening crowd.'

*   *   *

When she got back to her caravan there was a little note pinned to her door.

'Dr Thomas Murray requests the pleasure of Miss Nikki Gale for dinner at the White House. Cocktails 7.30 for dinner at 8. No need RSVP unless not convenient. Dress, semi-formal.'

Great! A chance to dress up again. Cocktails? And dinner? Dress semi-formal? She'd show him.

He had seen her in her ballgown at the Farmers' Ball—she didn't want to think of that now. She thought something shorter, something cool and elegant. She wouldn't wear tights—she never did unless she had to—but, yes, she had just the right dress in mind.

She had a couple of hours and there were few things more pleasurable than a long getting-ready session. She proposed to enjoy every minute.

First the shower and the hair-washing. Then Nikki sat dressed just in a towel and dried and brushed her hair till it shone. The body lotion kept for special occasions, lacy white underwear. She wondered if he might see it—and blushed at the thought. Then the dark blue dress that did so much for her hair and her skin. For once she would wear high heels. Well, moderately high. She didn't like to teeter about.

She put on lipstick and eye make-up with more care than usual. A cameo brooch that had been a twenty-first birthday present. At a quarter past seven she made a final brooding assessment and decided that she looked pretty good. She was ready for her cocktails.

With a shiver she hoped she'd read the signs right. If she got there and discovered that they were going to eat fish and chips from a take-away she would feel a bit of an idiot. She took a light wrap in case it turned chilly later and set off.

She had always loved the White House—it was her ideal dwelling. Far beyond her means, of course, but what she had always wanted. It was small enough to be manageable, large enough to have a family and a gracious style of living.

She loved her caravan, of course, but that was just a one-woman lifestyle. In time she would outgrow it.

Since she was formally dressed, she would call formally. No running across the back lawn like she would have in her slippers or bare feet. She took the lane to the side and out onto the main road and then walked up to the double front doors between their white pillars. It was exactly 7.30. She hoped again this was going to be the right outfit. She rang the doorbell.

The door opened at once and she knew instantly that she was wearing the right outfit. Tom was wearing a suit—not a dark doctor's suit but a light fawn linen suit. With it he wore a crisp blue shirt and a dark blue silk tie. He looked every inch the debonair man about town and she felt a momentary shiver of doubt. After all, this was Hambleton. But his welcome reassured her.

'Nikki, you look absolutely gorgeous.' He leaned forward to kiss her on the cheek. 'I've not seen that dress before, it really suits you. Come on in.'

They entered the panelled hall. Nikki had thought that the Rixes' furniture had never fitted in the White House, but it was unable to hide this first room's elegance.

He escorted her down the hall to the small back

study. This was obviously the room he was making his own. There were new medical books, the inevitable computer. He sat her in a large leather chair and said, 'I spent quite a bit of time in America—in a big hospital in Las Vegas, in fact. I learned a lot there—and one of the things was how to make a perfect Marguerita. I've got a pitcher here. Would you like to try one?'

'A real cocktail? I've only ever had Martini out of a bottle. Yes, please, I'd love one.'

On a silver tray was an ice-frosted pitcher, two glasses, some lemon slices and a saucer of salt. He dipped the rim of the glass in the salt, filled it from the pitcher and then added a slice of lemon.

She took the glass, sipped, blinked and sipped a second time. 'I don't think I'll ever drink a cocktail from a bottle again,' she said. 'This is heaven. Tell me, will dinner be as good?'

He sat opposite her and laughed. 'I hope so but I'm not sure.'

'You know, I don't know all that much about you. I'm learning all the time. Are you a wonderful cook as well as everything else?'

'Possibly not. This morning I bought a cookery book. This afternoon I bought all the necessary ingredients from the supermarket. And the last three hours I've spent cooking and thoroughly enjoying myself, book in one hand, stirring spoon in the other. So far my top culinary success has been a bacon and egg sandwich.' He looked thoughtful. 'Though I must say that was pretty good.'

'So this is part of your programme of self-development? To do as many new things as possible?'

'It certainly is. And why not? You can help me, there are lots of things I want to do. I've already started on some.'

He looked at her and she blushed.

They were to eat in the dining room. He'd pushed the big table to one side and found a small circular one. There was a pure white tablecloth, silver cutlery. There were lit candles on the table and the sideboard and the mantelpiece.

'I love candles,' she said dreamily. 'They're a bit dangerous in the van but I still love them. It's a light like no other.'

'I know. It's romantic. Would you like to sit here?'

The meal was marvellous. He had organized it so he didn't constantly have to jump up and down but could sit and chat to her. He had found a set of chafing dishes, so all the food could be kept warm on the sideboard. To start with there was a salmon and watercress salad with hot rolls. The main course was chicken in white wine with new potatoes and fresh vegetables. Then a fresh fruit salad and a cheese board. As they ate he kept her amused by describing the trials and tribulations of the cooking. 'The chicken was easiest,' he said with a grin. 'No problem with bones for an orthopaedics man.'

With the meal they drank a sparkling Saumur. There was no need to hurry. They sat at their ease, eating, drinking, chatting. They had time, she realised. Too much of life was spent in a hurry. The thing to do was make the most of the moment.

Finally they went back to the study, now smelling wonderfully of coffee. 'Before we sit down I'll help you wash up,' she offered, 'then you don't have it to worry about.'

He shook his head decisively. 'I want this evening to be perfect. There's no need to worry about the washing-up, I want it to be just you and me.' So they sat and drank coffee. He offered her a brandy. She refused and noticed that he didn't have one either.

Nikki felt content. There was that feeling of having eaten well but not too fully. And she was with the man she loved. What more could she ask for?

'Tell me about your day,' she said. 'How are you settling in?'

He laughed. 'I think I'm slowly being accepted by the locals. We had the usual number of holidaymakers, ill or injured because they were in a hurry. When will they learn to use sunblock? Only simple stuff, though. And I scored a couple from the town itself— one wanting advice on her arthritis, one needing a new prescription for hayfever. I hope I helped them.'

'So you don't mind moving from being a high-powered surgeon to simple prescriptions for simple illnesses?'

'Certainly not. What I like about Hambleton is that it's never just doctor and patient. It's never just an illness or an accident. There has to be a couple of sentences of gossip first.'

'It's to show you're part of the community. And don't forget, to a doctor gossip is invaluable.'

'I can see that. Now, I want to know about you. And I want to know about your day. What did you do that was interesting?'

Nikki thought for a moment. At heart she was an honest woman and she knew she had to tell him— even though he had wanted his story kept a secret. 'I called at the farm to see my parents. I told them I was seeing you. And my mother asked me what illness you were suffering from. She used to be a nurse, you know.'

'So you told her?' His voice was calm.

'Yes. She knew already, I think. But don't worry, neither of them will say a word to anyone.' She looked at him anxiously. 'Tom, you don't mind, do you?'

He reached for the brandy decanter, poured himself a small glass. 'I came here intending to have a quiet life, to keep my secret to myself. Only Joe was to know.' He sipped his brandy. 'I've been here a few weeks and three more people know.'

'Do you really mind?'

He mused for a while. 'I thought I would but I don't. In fact, it's almost a relief, a burden shared.'

'I want to share your burden,' she said. 'I know you wanted to keep it secret, and even to me you still laugh and joke about it. But it is a strain, isn't it?'

'Sometimes,' he replied slowly. 'But you are making things easier for me.'

Did he know how much that pleased her?

Tom went on, more cheerfully, 'So you told your parents about *us* did you?'

'Well, I said I was seeing you. And when I saw Dad and Ma together, and talked to them, I thought of something. Not the sort of thing you usually think about your parents. I thought that ultimately I wanted a marriage like theirs. A love like they've got. And even if the man I love is ill, it won't stand in the way!'

She realised she had raised her voice a little and wondered if she'd had too much wine. But Tom didn't seem to mind.

He reached over and took her hand. 'That's really something. But don't forget—we're on probation for the next three months. Just seeing how things will go.'

'I know how things will go,' she muttered.

'We'll have to see.' He grinned at her. 'Are we officially an item, then? This is something new for me. Am I now the boyfriend-in-title?'

Nikki thought about it. 'I guess you are. If it's a job you want.'

'So long as you remember the conditions, it's a job I want very much. Now, shouldn't I be invited to a formal tea with your parents? Wait for your dad to take me to one side and ask me about my financial prospects?'

'Forget the financial prospects. But as to coming to tea…are you doing anything next Sunday night?'

'I don't think so. I'll spend it with you if I can. Why?'

'That'll be the day you could come to tea and meet my family.'

They were sitting side by side now on the great leather couch that was the one piece of furniture that Nikki really liked. Tom put down his coffee-cup and slipped an arm round her shoulder. She leaned against him, putting her arm round his waist. 'Are you happy?' she asked.

He seemed to consider the question. 'More than I could have imagined a few weeks ago,' he said. 'I guess I got tired of being the tough man who could take anything that life dished out. Coming here, meeting you has made even…even ordinary things seem special. Each day is something new, something exciting. You've taught me that.'

She giggled. 'Sure it's not the country air, and new experiences like falling out of trees and rubbing brasses?'

His hand slid down her side. 'I've got better things to rub than brasses.'

'That's not rubbing, that's stroking. Don't stop, it's lovely.'

'Tell me what you get out of being in love, Nikki?'

'It's like you said. Everything ordinary seems so much better. I get a bigger kick out of my work. I know I'm going to see you soon and I feel content.'

'And the future?'

'We have a future, Tom, I know we have.'

He hadn't stopped stroking and it was making her feel both sleepy and excited, an odd combination. He bent to kiss her and said, 'Your eyes are closing. Are you ready for bed?'

'I thought you'd never ask,' she said softly.

It was Sunday evening and they were visiting her parents for tea.

'I'm nervous,' Tom said, and Nikki guessed he was only half joking.

'Don't be. They'll all love you and you'll be something else for them to gossip about.' They had to park at the far end of the yard as there were another five vehicles there already.

'I've never taken a man to see my parents for Sunday tea,' she said. 'Lots of friends when I was younger, but never a man I might be…well, interested in.'

'You're frightening me,' he said amiably. 'All these people will look at me and whisper about me.' He looked as she casually waved at the group of adults by the kitchen door, the children running around the yard. 'Is this a special party for something?'

'Just Sunday tea. Every second Sunday some of the family drop in. I've got two older brothers with families, there are some cousins and a few relationships I'm not quite sure of. It's all very free and easy. Come and meet everyone.'

He blinked. 'This is worse than being interviewed by a gang of consultants.'

'Auntie Nikki, Auntie Nikki! Come and see! The chicken has just had babies and they're all yellow!' Two tiny children in tiny wellingtons rushed up and grabbed her by the hands.

'We have to start with the grand farmyard tour,' Nikki explained. 'Let's see the baby chickens first.'

Tom fitted in well with her relations—as she'd known he would. The children were fed first, then all the family gathered round the great table in the kitchen. They ate and Tom listened to stories about farming. Then he went round the stock with her father and her two brothers in a pair of borrowed boots. Meanwhile Nikki fended off enquiries from the assorted female relations about how serious things were, and how nice he was.

'You'll have trouble picking bridesmaids,' one sister-in-law said with a sly smile. 'I calculate that there's at least ten little girls who will think they're entitled to a long dress and to walk up the aisle with you.'

'There's a long way to go before I even think about bridesmaids,' said Nikki. 'For the moment we're just seeing how it goes.' She knew from the expressions around her that she had fooled nobody.

No one stayed too late. There were children to be put to bed, work to be done the next morning. When they drove away Nikki felt they'd had a good evening.

'I enjoyed myself,' Tom said, 'I really did. It made me feel as if I'd been left out of something—I've never had a family like that. It must be marvellous.'

'It is,' she said. 'Anyone marrying a Gale doesn't get a wife or husband. They get a ready-made entire family.'

'I think I'd like that.'

He's coming round, she thought, he's coming round. She had known that loving him would be hard, but now she had hope. The fixed ideas he had seemed to be wavering a little.

CHAPTER SEVEN

IT WASN'T hard to keep secrets in Hambleton—it was impossible. They were both busy, but they went out together once or twice—for a drink in the Tinsley Arms or a walk along the river—and the entire place knew about them. Nikki accepted this as normal. Tom was a bit bewildered by it.

It was Thursday, and they were having a coffee in the doctors' lounge at the surgery. He had just finished his morning appointments and she had called in to have a prescription signed. He snatched a kiss and said he thought nurses in uniform were wonderful.

'All nurses?'

'Well, some fill the uniform better than others.' He dextrously avoided her punch.

'I've seen seven locals this morning,' he said. 'Three of them told me they'd seen us out together. Quite nicely, of course, but there was a silence afterwards so I could explain if I wanted.'

'And what did you explain?'

'I said that I was new to the area, that you were just showing me round the place. No one said anything but I don't think anyone believed me.'

Nikki laughed. 'I'm afraid this isn't anonymous London. If you're a doctor or a nurse then you're part of the public domain. People are entitled to be curious about your private life. Do you really mind?'

'It takes a bit of getting used to—but not really.

This morning I had old Miss Perkins in—she saw us down by the river. She said she taught you in junior school—you were a good girl even then. A very hard worker. Miss Perkins was obviously wondering if I was good enough for you.'

Nikki grinned. 'She was a terror. Very strict. I was scared stiff of her. But could she teach! She was the only unmarried teacher in the school, though she had been engaged once.'

Tom nodded. 'I saw the ring. It had a little diamond—but it looks very worn now.'

'My grandfather told me about her before he died,' Nikki said. 'Miss Perkins was engaged to a soldier, a Sergeant Keith Collins. He was killed at the Normandy landings. His name's on the war memorial by the church. Every Remembrance Sunday you'll see Miss Perkins there with a wreath for him. She's never forgotten him, never looked at another man.'

Nikki's voice died away, realising she'd talked herself into a trap. She knew what Tom would think. If they got engaged or married and he died...how would she cope? Looking up at him, she said, 'That's the story. You're not to take any lessons from it, it's nothing to do with us.'

He nodded. 'They're not us. They were in love, I think we are. They were engaged, we're not. Our relationship is on hold, we had an agreement.'

'I know what I want,' she said fiercely, 'and I think I know what you want. You can't make decisions for me Tom, we've already talked about that.'

But she wasn't happy. Although he didn't reply there was a spark of determination in his eye. Sadly, she realised that there were some things she just couldn't move him on.

* * *

Another lovely hot day. This was turning into a summer to remember. As Nikki drove to an outlying village, all the car windows open to provide a draught of cooling air, she wondered what it would be like in London in this heat. Tom had told her that the capital was usually warmer than up here. Today in London would be sheer purgatory!

She was visiting Charlie Dove, a six-year-old who had measles. He had a slight temperature and was restless in the heat. Nikki showed his mother how to bathe the little face and body in lukewarm water, and after a while his restlessness subsided.

Then her mobile rang. She excused herself and went into the street to answer it. It was Tom. There was the usual little flutter that she felt when she heard his voice.

'Nikki, where are you?' His voice was calm, efficient. This was something serious. She explained where she was.

'Good, you're handy. I've just had a phone call from Mary Dunmore. She's had a fall, she can hardly move. She won't complain but I get the feeling that it's something serious. I'm on my way there—can you meet me?'

'Of course. Shouldn't we send for an ambulance?'

He laughed. 'I suggested that. She said no way was she leaving George. I think we might have to do some heavy-duty persuading.'

'I'll be there in twenty minutes.'

In fact, she arrived after Tom. Inside she found Mary lying on the settee, her leg raised, her face white. She was holding a mug of tea, obviously made by Tom.

'I don't like this tea,' she said as Nikki entered. 'It's too sweet.'

Nikki guessed what it was. 'Your blood sugar's down, Mary,' she said gently, 'and you're suffering from shock. The tea'll make you feel better.'

She turned to George, who was sitting in his usual chair, his Dickens lying by him. 'How do you feel, George?'

'Helpless,' George said, 'and I don't like it.' The words were strong but there was a quaver in his voice that hadn't been there before.

Tom came out of the kitchen and took Nikki to one side. 'Her leg's broken,' he said. 'I can't tell without X-rays but I think it's a really bad complex fracture of the femur. I've sent for an ambulance. Mary will have to be admitted to hospital. All we've got to do is get her to accept that.'

Nikki turned. 'What happened, Mary?

'I thought I could help George move. Usually he can help himself a bit but today he was too heavy for me. He fell back in his chair, I fell over the fender.'

Nikki looked at the high fender and winced. It must have been agonising.

Mary went on, 'Now, strap this up so I can get about. I can't go to hospital, I've got to look after George.'

'It can't be done, Mary,' Tom said gently. 'I'm a bones man myself, and your leg is in a mess. You could be bleeding internally—and that's really serious if it's not treated. By serious, I mean you could die.' The stark words echoed in the dark room.

'What about George?' Mary asked. 'How can he manage without me?'

'I'll personally see that he's well looked after,' Nikki said quickly. 'He can go to that nursing home in—'

'No nursing home! George and I have been together all these years and I won't leave—'

'No, Mary,' George said suddenly, 'I want to go to the nursing home. You've got to be strong, like I have. You can't look after me now. And how do you think I'd feel if you...if you left me for good?'

There was silence for a while. Nikki wondered if Mary would cry, she could guess what the woman was going through. But Mary was tough. She didn't cry. 'All right,' she said after a while, 'I'll go to hospital and George can go to this nursing home. You did say that it was run by Agnes Garthwaite's daughter.' She had to struggle to keep her voice calm but she added, 'Nikki, you'll visit him there and see that he's all right, won't you? And you'll come and tell me?'

'Of course I will,' said Nikki. 'You've made the right decision, Mary.'

In the distance they could hear the ambulance siren.

Nikki was an organiser, she knew what needed to be done. She packed a bag for Mary and brought it down just as the paramedics loaded her into the ambulance. 'Don't worry, Mary,' she said, 'I won't leave George till I know he's OK.' But by now Mary was happy to leave all the arrangements to her. She had held up long enough, her weary body was now paying the price.

Nikki took Tom to one side and whispered to him, 'Do you want me to see to everything else here? It's a nurse's job really, and since I know them it'll be easy for me.'

He thought for a moment. 'Seems the best thing. I've got a few cases I have to look at still. Now, shall we have supper together?'

'I'd like to cook for you.' There was something she'd been considering for a while. 'You know there's a barbecue pit at the back of the White House? Could I use it?'

'You don't need to ask.'

'Right, I'll see you there later. I'll call at the supermarket and get all that's needed, and it'll be my treat.'

'Leave the wine to me. Now, in here...' He pulled her into the kitchen and kissed her. 'That's till later,' he said.

When Tom and the ambulance had left, Nikki first made sure that George was comfortable and had been fed. For a while she sat chatting to him, getting him to reminisce about the days when he'd been able to farm. Only when she thought that he was calmer did she start on the long list of things that had to be done.

Technically, Social Services should attend to George so first Nikki phoned and left a message about what she was doing for Marion Watts, the senior social worker. She and Marion worked well together. Marion was an ex-nurse and they understood each other.

Then Nikki phoned the nursing home to check that there was a vacancy. Yes, they could always find a place for George Dunmore. She phoned the farmer who worked the land. He'd keep an eye on the farmhouse and buildings. Then there were documents to be sorted, a couple of cases packed for George.

It was time to go. Nikki was much stronger than Mary and she had no difficulty helping George into his wheelchair. They moved into the yard, and she left him there a minute as she brought the car a little nearer. 'Just a half-hour trip and you'll be there, George,' she said.

He showed no sign of moving. 'One more minute,' he said. She saw him look at the house, the buildings, the fields, the surrounding hills. He stared at them as if he had never seen them before—or perhaps he thought he would never see them again.

'You'll be back, George,' she urged. 'Don't worry, you'll be back. This is only for a while.'

'Are you sure?' he asked, and Nikki felt a touch of guilt. She had been thinking that the old couple shouldn't stay in this desolate place much longer.

'We'll get you comfortable and Mary's leg mended and then we'll think about the future.'

'Maybe. I'll say goodbye to the place anyway. Now, can you help me into that car?'

Fortunately they were expecting her and George at the nursing home. There were people there who knew him and one resident had worked for him in the past. Nikki left them chatting quite happily as she had a few words with Doreen Garthwaite, the matron.

'He'll be happy here,' said Doreen. 'He and Mary have been on their own for too long. But we'll make a fuss of him.'

'I'll ring you when I have any news of Mary,' Nikki promised. Then she drove back to the surgery. There were more forms to fill in and Joe would certainly want to know what was happening. It was turn-

ing into a hard afternoon, but in some ways a satisfying one.

Finally she was finished. Now she could live for
herself a little. She drove to the supermarket, bought
rolls, pre-prepared salad, marinade, chicken breasts
and kebabs. Once home she took off her uniform,
showered and dressed in shirt and shorts. Then she
put all her purchases on a tray and went into the
White House garden.

As she walked she could smell woodsmoke, exciting and evocative, reminding her of camping trips
with the Guides when she was much younger. Tom
must have already lit the barbecue—that would save
time.

It was a good barbecue pit, Nikki would have
loved one like it herself. As well as the barbecue
itself, there was a bricked floor, a table and benches,
even a water supply and sink in a corner. Just the
thing for a family picnic.

She saw Tom and, as always, her heart skipped a
beat. He was also in shorts and a polo shirt and he
looked so…well, so good. At present he had that
earnest expression she had seen before, and he was
looking doubtfully at the charcoal. He picked up a
stick and she said, 'You're not supposed to poke it.
You're supposed to let it settle.'

'I think I'm a primitive man. When I see an open
fire I feel this great urge to blow and poke and fiddle.
I've decided that modern gas and electric fires are a
poor substitute. They keep you warm all right but
there's no satisfaction in adjusting a thermostat.'

'The White House still has a couple of open
grates,' she said with a smile. 'Perhaps in winter you
could light a fire in one.'

'That would be fun. Now, you've had a long, hot day. Mary Dunmore is fine. But before you tell me about George, sit here a minute and have a glass of this.'

On the table was a bottle of wine in a bowl of ice and two glasses. He poured her a glass and sat by her side. Then he kissed her—a gentle kiss.

'The practice is very lucky, having you,' he said. 'You've got more than nursing skills, you've got people skills. You handled George and Mary really well.'

'All part of a day's work,' she told him.

'Seeing them together made me think. It was so hard to part them, neither of them could bear it. Losing someone you love—even for a while—is always difficult.'

She drank some of the wine and felt better at once. 'Don't try to get any kind of lesson out of this afternoon,' she said. 'Mary and George aren't Nikki and Tom. And they have had fifty years together.'

He smiled sadly. 'The very fact you need to mention it means that you're aware of any lesson there might be. Now, what have you brought? I'm ravenous.'

Nikki had long ago decided that barbecues were great fun so long as you accepted that they were never going to be anything but a slapdash meal. Smoke got everywhere, the fat splashed your arms, there was always some bit of the meat that was charred beyond belief. And that was part of the charm.

'Have you ever been to a well-organised barbecue?' she asked Tom as she fished on the coals for a piece of meat that had slipped through the grill.

'I've been to far worse ones than this,' he said. 'You look incredibly efficient.'

'Just wait and see what it tastes like.' But she liked his compliment. And she had also been to more badly organised affairs.

There was a good bed of hot coals. She put on the meat, then buttered rolls and put the salad into a big bowl. Then she drank more wine. And as they sat and laughed together she felt the strains of the day disappearing. It was good just to be with Tom.

He told her stories of working on the orthopaedic ward, of trying to get young tearaway motorcyclists to lie still when all they wanted to do was to be up and out. 'I tried everything. I even got a yoga teacher to come round to try to teach them calmness and wisdom and inner serenity. But mostly just to lie still till their bones knitted.'

She thought this was a very interesting idea. 'Did it work?' she asked.

'I'm not sure. It might have in time. But after four weeks I saw her arrive at the hospital on a big motorbike, wearing tight black leathers. So I just had to sack her.'

'I don't believe you!'

'True, entirely true! In fact, it wasn't the leathers and the bike that put me off. It was the tattooing.'

Yes, it was good to be with him. She shared his sense of humour, they relaxed so easily together.

In time the meal was done and she served it on the paper plates she had brought. They sat and ate as the evening waned, sometimes talking, sometimes content to be silent. Eventually it grew dark.

'There are signs of barbecuing all over you,' he said tenderly brushing her cheek with a finger. 'You are far too dirty to get clean in that tiny shower of yours. Why don't we take all this in and then you could stay and have a bath in my bathroom?'

'I've seen that bath, it's big. In fact, it's big enough for two of us. You're also dirty—you could join me.'

He considered that. 'All right. And would you like to stay the night?'

'Shall I fetch my nightie?'

'You didn't need it last night, you won't tonight. We'll manage somehow.'

'I'll be happy to stay, then, kind sir.'

It was an enormous bath. The taps were in the middle and two people could lie down facing each other. If you twisted a knob, jets of air bubbled through the water. When Nikki saw it she thought it the last word in luxury—not decadence but luxury. What could be better than sharing a bath with someone you loved?

Nikki undressed quickly, poured foaming stuff into the water and climbed in. A minute later Tom came into the bathroom in his dressing-gown. She was still a little shy and she sank further into the foam and looked away as he took off the gown and climbed in with her. Then she giggled. 'What do you think you're doing with your foot?' she asked.

He looked at her innocently. 'Just trying to find the soap.'

'Well, you certainly won't find it there.' But he still didn't stop.

They lay there and had a last glass of wine each. She felt the warm water washing away her cares and she knew that he felt the same.

He said, 'This is too good to give up. I need you and this for the rest of my life.'

She was happy. She was persuading him.

Nikki had agreed that for three months they wouldn't think or talk about Tom's illness. Tom hadn't mentioned it once himself. But she didn't think much of the idea that if you ignored problems they would sort themselves out. She wanted to know all that she could about Hodgkin's disease then she could make up her own mind about things. She knew Tom could be awkward, determined to do what he thought right no matter what other people felt. Well, she could be awkward and determined, too.

The next day was Friday, she waited till Tom was out of the surgery and then went to see Joe. 'What's the best book you've got that tells me about Hodgkin's disease, Joe?'

Of course, he knew at once why she wanted to know. 'You know about Tom. Please, don't try to involve yourself, Nikki. You leave that to the experts who can maintain the necessary detachment. Remember, a doctor who treats himself has a fool for a patient.'

'I'm involved already, Joe. I'm not detached, I'm very involved and I just have to know.'

He sighed. 'I didn't want this. Tom's a great doctor but this is the kind of problem we could all do without. But here, these two books will give you a start. And remember, Nikki, you don't learn medicine from a book!'

He unlocked a cupboard and took out two massive tomes. 'These are reasonably up to date. But medicine—especially in an area like oncology—changes every month. Don't make any decisions based on what you read.'

'I just want to know! I can't stand being left in the dark. I need to understand, it all seems so unfair.'

'As a nurse you should know that a lot of life is unfair. I hope you don't get hurt in this, Nikki. He's a determined man.' Then he was gone.

She had an hour free. The surgery was largely deserted so she took her two heavy books into the lounge and started to read. She already had some knowledge of the subject, had indeed nursed on an oncology ward when she'd been training. But she wanted to know more.

Hodgkin's disease was a cancer of the lymphatic glands. It was comparatively rare and no one really knew the cause. If detected in time it could be treated, by radiotherapy or chemotherapy. Prognosis was usually quite good. But if it had metastasised—colonised other parts of the body—prognosis wasn't so good. And it wasn't just a simple disease. There were a bewildering number of sub-types, variations, stages. And the risk of each was different.

'I hope your interest in that topic is professional and not personal.'

She looked up with a start. She had been engrossed in what she was reading, it was fascinating but not easy. Somehow Tom had entered the lounge without her hearing him and had walked across to look over her shoulder. He wasn't pleased. His voice was cold, his face set and angry.

'No, it's personal,' she said. 'I've got an interest and I want to know what I'm dealing with.'

'I thought we had an agreement. For three months we forget about any illness and at the end of that time we think again. Now I find you're going behind my back.'

His tone was still unforgiving, but now she was over the surprise of seeing him she was getting angry herself. 'I don't like the idea of just waiting for things to happen. I'd rather fight. I want to know what's possible and what isn't. You've told me a bit but I need to know more.'

'No, you don't! I know plenty and I don't like it!'

He walked over to the window and stared out of it as if he were seeking an answer there. 'But now I don't want to think, I just want to be. I was looking forward to three months out of my life when I didn't need to worry, three months of pure happiness, if you like. I've spent the past eighteen months wondering what's going to happen to me, Nikki, and apart from anything else it's tiring.'

He came back to sit by her and flicked the book shut with his finger. His voice was calmer. 'You've brought me a happiness I didn't know was possible. Perhaps it's for only a few months, but it was a gift I never expected. And to find you worrying about what might happen, it spoils it for me.'

'I don't want to spoil anything! But not knowing, it's more than I can stand. Just answer me a quick question, Tom. From what I've just read, the prognosis of Hodgkin's disease is usually quite hopeful. Why are you so pessimistic?'

'It's a disease that comes in a variety of forms. It just so happens I've got a particularly dangerous form. If you want, I could take you through all the details. I've spent hours reading through the subject, trying to find some hope. And I haven't succeeded.'

'Oh, Tom!' The very thought was almost more

than she could bear. Her voice faltering, she said, 'I just wanted to know things, then I could understand, even could make plans.'

'I don't want you to make plans! There's nothing to be done. Don't worry, I'm getting the best, the very best medical attention there is. And my consultant will tell you the same as I do. We just have to wait and see.'

'Tom! You mustn't hurt me like this!' she sobbed.

'I don't want to. Because hurting you is hurting myself.'

He stood and walked over to an easy chair, sat there with his arms folded. It seemed as if he had deliberately put a distance between them, his body language rejecting her. She knew she couldn't walk across to him. He had set himself apart.

'I was going to keep this from you,' he said. 'Perhaps it wasn't a good idea.'

'Whatever you're talking about, keeping it from me wasn't a good idea. I want to know everything.'

'Perhaps. You know I suffer from Hodgkin's disease. I've had treatment and now I'm in remission. But that might not last. There's a one in three chance that I will die. Think of that, Nikki. At the beginning of every year I know that there's a one in three chance I won't see the end of it. But I can stand that, there's still a two in three chance that I'll survive and I feel quite hopeful. Imagine how I feel if there's someone I love and I know they have to go through that awful wondering, too. That hurts. In some ways I was happier when I didn't have you, then I knew that my illness only affected one person.'

'That's terrible! And I don't care if you are ill, I can take it.'

'Perhaps you can. But I don't know if I can. I'm being selfish now. It's hard to know you might die. It's even harder to know that you're hurting someone you love.'

Nikki had never thought about it as starkly as he had put it. What more could she say? 'Please, Tom, I just want a hug.'

So he hugged her and she drew comfort from him. Perhaps he was upset himself. He held her so tightly at first that she felt the breath being squeezed from her lungs. She could feel the muscles of his arm, his shoulders. Surely all this masculine strength couldn't be ill! No way could she bear the thought. But she would have to.

After some time her sobbing ceased and she eased herself away from him. He offered her a handkerchief and she wiped her face. Then she said, 'Remember in the church when you rubbed that brass? You said that the couple's love had lasted for hundreds of years. Well, that's a long time. I don't want hundreds of years—but I want our love to last for longer than three months. And it's going to.'

Tom nodded wearily. 'You sound like I used to feel.'

There was silence for a moment and they both heard the sound of footsteps in the corridor outside. Then a receptionist put her head round the door and said, 'Dr Murray? We've got a lady in the waiting room. I suppose it's a bit of an emergency, so if you've got a minute…'

'I'll come at once,' said Tom.

Nikki waited till he had left then opened the book again. She needed to know. Then she could fight.

*   *   *

On Sunday she decided to spend at her parents' farm. It wasn't a Sunday when the family would come to tea, but she felt that she needed a day in the open air. Not that it would be relaxing.

'Your mother's gone visiting in Harrogate,' her father said when she phoned. 'If you want to help me, I'm going to rebuild the wall on the top pasture.'

'Just what I need. Something hard and sweaty and mindless. For the moment I'm tired of ill people.'

She wasn't really tired of ill people but a change would be good for her. It would be good to get back to where she had been brought up, to remember the certainties of life as it used to be.

It was Tom's turn to remain at the surgery. Throughout the summer Joe liked there to be a doctor available at the weekends. Nikki didn't want to be away from him but knew that a few hours by herself might be good for her, might enable her to look more clearly at what decision she had to make.

He father was an expert dry-stone waller. She had learned a little herself, but he was the one who could work at speed. It was her job to pull down the bits of wall that were falling and pile up the stones handy for him. Then he came and replaced them. Whatever the gap, there always seemed to be a stone of just the right size and shape. It was marvellous!

They worked in the sun together, she enjoying the unaccustomed exercise, the chance to try muscles too often not used. And as they worked they talked—casually, as they used to do.

'So why did you need to come here to work?' he asked eventually. 'And are you tired of all ill people or just one?'

This was typical of her father. He had been able to read her since she was a little girl.

'I suppose it's Tom. And I'm not tired of him—just the opposite. But I'm tired of thinking about his illness. I think he's wonderful, Dad, I really do. It's just that, well, he doesn't think it right that I should want to have a relationship with him when his future is so uncertain.'

'Well, you could say that shows he's a caring man. He's trying to consider what's best for you and not himself. But you think you know better?'

'Whose side are you on?' Her voice was sharp.

Her father looked surprised at the question. 'Your side, of course. And perhaps Tom's, too. I'm just suggesting you should at least think about what he's said. Try to do it calmly, weigh up both sides of the argument.'

'There is no argument, I know that…' she flared up, and then saw him smiling at her. 'All right, I'll try and be calm.'

In fact, it was a good exercise for her. It made her thinking more pointed, more exact. After a while she asked, 'If you were Tom and I were Mum, what would you say and do?'

Her father heaved a great stone onto the top of the wall, where it fitted perfectly. He looked at it gloomily. 'You know how to ask hard questions, don't you?' he said. 'How can I answer that?'

'You can answer it honestly. Dad, I need some help. I don't want you to tell me what to do, I want you to help me decide myself.'

Nikki knew better than to worry when he didn't reply at once. He had always been like this, willing to take time to consider so that his answer would be the right one. Quite different from her quicksilver mother—though usually they agreed on everything in the end.

'If I were Tom and you were your mum,' he said, 'I'd like to think that I'd say what Tom is saying now. But inside I'd desperately hope that you wouldn't pay any attention to me. But, like you said, this must be your decision and you have to consider carefully. So think long and hard.'

It wasn't something she wanted to think about. But she knew her father was right, it had to be considered. So she considered it as calmly and as coolly as she was able and at the end of five minutes she said, 'I still want to take the chance if he'll let me. I know that if he ever asked me to marry him, I would.'

Her father made no comment. It was her decision. Only she could make it, and she had thought about it. After a while he said, 'I remember the first time you stayed up all night. You were six.'

It seemed an odd thing to say. 'Why is that important? I can't even remember it.'

'I think you can. We were lambing and it was a really bad week. One of my ewes had died and I brought her lamb home. Only a few hours old, I was sure she would die. But I showed you how to feed her, using a baby's bottle, and you made her a bed in the bottom drawer of the Aga. You stayed up all night, feeding that lamb.'

'I remember now.' Nikki smiled at the memory. 'The lamb lived.'

'That's right. I didn't think it would, but the lamb lived.'

'Is that supposed to be some kind of lesson for me? Some kind of encouragement?'

Her father looked at her innocently. 'What can you mean? I was only remembering something from when you were a little girl. Now, I think this wall should hold. We've done a good day's work.'

She rose, feeling the stiffness in her shoulders. 'I think we have,' she said.

She decided not to stay at the farm. Instead, she would go back to her caravan, perhaps call Tom. By the time she got back he would have finished at the surgery. Perhaps she would tell him she'd thought about their parting and had decided it wasn't a good idea. Or maybe she'd tell him about the lamb that she'd nursed—the lamb that had lived.

It was a golden evening. She hadn't changed at the farm, she'd come home in her work clothes and she was hot, sticky and tired. So first of all she would have a shower.

The evening had turned even more golden as she opened the back gates and drove into her parking space. There was her patio, her white table and chairs. And there was Tom, sitting on one of the chairs, waiting for her.

'Tom!' She jumped out of her car, ran across to him. Perhaps she was stiffer than she'd thought, perhaps it was just one of those accidents. But somehow her ankle turned under her and she fell full length— her side slamming into a brick on the edge of the lawn. Pain lanced through her and she knew she screamed. She must have broken a rib or something.

She rolled off the brick and the pain came back, worse than ever. Perhaps she lost consciousness for a moment or two. When she managed to open her eyes Tom was leaning over her, his hands holding her shoulders. A distant part of her mind noted that, though he sounded like a doctor, he looked like a lover. There was a wealth of concern in his eyes. But for the moment he was all efficiency.

'Nikki, you're going to be all right. Now, don't try to move. Just lie there, don't breathe too deeply and the pain will go after a while. OK? Don't move. I'll stay here with you and hold your hand. You're going to be all right.'

So she closed her eyes again and did as he said. Her breathing grew slowly easier and the pain in her side got easier to bear. And she was comforted when Tom held her hand.

'Right, now, did you hurt your head at all or your neck? I didn't think so, you fell onto soft ground.'

'My head and neck are fine. I feel silly. I shouldn't have fallen there. I've—'

'Don't worry. Just tell me where it does hurt.'

'I fell on that brick. I thought at first that my ribs were broken, but now I'm not sure.'

'Hmm. Can you feel your legs—will you move them a little?'

'My legs are fine—look. I haven't injured my spine, Tom. It's just my side.'

'Well, just lie there and I'll see what I can find.'

Nikki felt him easing up the edge of her shirt, pulling down the waistband of her jeans. There were his fingers, as gentle as a mother's, stroking, pressing gently. 'Ow,' she said, and repeated a short time later, 'Ow.' But it didn't really hurt.

'I doubt if there are any ribs broken,' he murmured. 'I think just a bad bruise. Now, I'm going to ease you up and we'll see if you can walk.' He helped her upright, and though the pain jabbed back she felt she could take it.

'I've been at the farm,' she said. 'I was dog tired and I was going to have a shower and then phone you and…' To her horror she heard her voice tremble. She wasn't hurt that badly!

'I don't think a shower. I'm going to help you over to my place and you can have a bath. You need to be able to stretch out. If I put my arm round you do you think you can make it?'

'I fell over. I didn't break my neck. This isn't a major accident.'

He grinned. 'There's my Nikki coming back. Come on, it's not far.'

He took her to his bathroom and although she said she wanted to get undressed herself, he made her promise to leave the door unlocked. 'I'll give you a couple of minutes and I'll bring you the traditional sweet tea.' Then he frowned and for a moment was a doctor again. 'One thing, see if there's any trace of blood in your urine.'

'Good idea. I will.' She was pretty sure her kidneys hadn't been ruptured, but it was as well to be sure.

The warm water was good for her. She inspected the injured side. There was going to be a bruise there and it would be hard to bend for a few days, but she decided there was no serious damage. So she lay there and after a few minutes Tom brought her tea. 'Aren't you having one?' she asked, so he fetched one for himself.

'Medical assistance doesn't usually involve sitting on the side of the bath,' he told her. 'It's not part of my doctor's training.'

'Well, I'm glad you're there. You know I've spent

the day walling with my father? That's why I'm so stiff, probably why I tripped over.'

He moved behind her, put his hands on each side of her neck and felt the muscles of her shoulders. 'These are knotted hard. You can get out now and we'll do something about them.'

It was odd. Not two days before she had shared this bath with him, had been completely happy for him to see her naked body. But now things were different and she felt shy. 'You've got your clothes on,' she said.

'I refuse to practise any kind of medicine stark naked. I don't know the exact rules, but I'm sure the BMA says that patients can be naked but that doctors have to be dressed.'

'But you're not practising medicine!'

'Oh, yes, I am,' he said. 'Or at least I'm going to. Now, here's a big towel. I'll help you up and you can wrap it round you.'

He led her to his bedroom—the place where they had made love so ecstatically two days before. Nikki gave a little squeak as he flicked the towel from round her and spread it out on the bed. 'Lie out on that,' he said. 'Lie out on your front and just try to relax.'

'What are you going to—?'

He gently pushed her forward. 'Just do as you're told.'

So she did. She felt strangely vulnerable, but she knew all would be well. He bent over and she knew he was inspecting her side again, his fingers cool against her water-warmed flesh.

'Not too much damage, I think,' he said, 'so now

we'll see to this stiffness. I thought all farmer's daughters were big and strong and never got tired.'

'I am and I don't,' she murmured. 'Well, just a bit.'

There was the smell of something floral and pleasant, and then the feel of a liquid on the nape of her neck. Tom brushed it downwards and then onto the muscles of her back and upper arms. Then he started to massage her back.

It was heavenly! His hands seemed to have a life of their own, stroking, rubbing, pummelling, squeezing. The fatigue and stiffness in her muscles drained away, leaving her with a feeling of incredible lightness. And she felt so sleepy! He poured more oil onto her legs and his strong hands moved down from thighs to ankles, coaxing the weary muscles out of their stiffness. Then there was each arm. It was bliss.

Finally he eased her over onto her back. 'Have you finished now?' she asked.

'All finished.'

'Then I think I'll go to sleep.'

She felt him kiss her on her forehead, and with a contented sigh, she drifted off.

CHAPTER EIGHT

WHEN Nikki woke later on, she was ravenous. Tom brought a meal up on a tray and they shared that and then she went to sleep again. And in the morning she felt fine. Her side was still stiff, but she could live with it. And she had to start work, they both did.

After that she often stayed the night with him in the White House. On occasion he would come and stay with her in the caravan. But they were still taking things easy, being careful with each other. There was no suggestion that she should move into the White House with him. Whatever they had, they had to take it very slowly.

She still tried to find out as much as possible about his disease, but she never mentioned it to him and he never talked about it. She knew that this was because of their agreement—to have three months in which nothing was said. She thought he was enjoying the time but still she wondered what he thought at night, if he ever dreaded what might come. To her he was perfectly calm and happy. But were there thoughts that she knew nothing of?

A week later, on Monday and Tuesday, Nikki went on a two-day course in Durham to learn all about the latest techniques in treating diabetes. One of the good things about nursing now was that as soon as there were new developments on drugs or treatments, there was usually a course about them. In the past few

years she'd been to a dozen courses on subjects rang-
ing from giving injections to the latest theories on
palliative care. And she'd learned from all of them.
This course was no exception, she'd have to visit
Penny Pink and tell her about it.

She made good time driving back and called in at
the surgery. She wanted to report in to Joe and perhaps arrange to have a meal with Tom later. They'd
agreed that she wouldn't phone him. Two days
wasn't long.

But Tom wasn't in the surgery. She was told that
he'd gone to Leeds. When he heard that she'd arrived, Joe sent word that she was to wait for him in
the doctors' lounge. Nikki felt the first stirrings of
apprehension.

'What's wrong with Tom?' she burst out when Joe
came into the lounge.

Joe came over and put his arm round her shoulders. 'We don't know yet. It might be nothing. But
he and I...and his consultant thought it better if he
went into hospital for tests.'

'Tests? What sort of tests?' Then she asked the
question she had been hiding from. 'Has his cancer
come back?'

'It's possible,' said Joe heavily, 'and it's also possible that it hasn't.' He looked at his watch. 'If you
want to drive down to see him, you could set off
now. There'll be a bed for you at the hospital if you
want it.'

Nikki was struggling to grasp what she had just
heard. Of course she knew from her reading that this
kind of thing could happen. It *could* happen. But
she'd never thought that it would. It had just been a
vague possibility, like being run over or winning the

lottery. She now realised as well that, in spite of her earlier brave words, she was just not capable of dealing with this. The horror was almost too much for her. What if he'd had a relapse?

'Thanks, Joe,' she muttered, 'I'll pack a couple more things and set off at once.'

'I trained as a nurse, I've worked in hospitals. In my time I've been in dozens of wards,' Nikki said to Tom. 'A hospital should be like a second home to me. But I'm sitting here and I don't feel at home at all.'

It was just something to say. She sat in the side ward and looked at him in bed and felt she just couldn't cope.

'Sometimes when I've been nursing I've had patients' relations turn on me, shout at me as if the illness was my fault. Now I know why. I'm powerless and it makes me feel so angry. Is there anything I can do for you, Tom?'

'You're doing something for me just by being here,' he said gently. 'I would have asked Joe to tell you not to come, but I knew you'd pay no attention. And I'm glad you came. How was the course?'

'Never mind the course! I didn't drive down here to tell you about my course! I drove down here because I love you and…' Somehow she stopped herself. 'My getting angry is helping you to make up your mind about something, isn't it?'

'I've had a chance to do a lot of thinking, Nikki.'

She looked at him. 'I've been talking to the ward sister,' she said. 'She thinks that this is just a false alarm. They just have to make certain with the tests and then you'll be back at work in a week.'

'I know that,' he said, and smiled at her. She didn't like it. It seemed as if he was mocking her, as if he knew what she was really thinking and had out-thought her already. They both knew that what the sister had said was only half-true.

'People like me worry all the time,' he went on. 'One of the signs of an upsurge in the disease again is a lymph gland getting swollen so at any time of the night or day you wonder, and you touch at a lymph gland. For most people it's hard to tell, but I'm not most people, I'm a doctor. There was a swelling in my neck. I came in here, had assorted tests and a biopsy. It appears that there's nothing wrong—the gland was swollen for some other reason.'

'So there's no need to worry,' she said. 'You come back to work, we both carry on as we were doing before.'

'No. I was foolish before, I was living in cloud-cuckoo-land. The cancer is there—we can't just ignore it. This time it was a false alarm. The next time it might be another false alarm, and the time after that. But we'll always both be wondering—what if this time it's for real? I'm a doctor, you're a nurse. We *know* what the chances are.'

'I can stand it if you can,' Nikki muttered.

'Can you? I don't know if I can.' He reached out and took her hand. 'D'you know what I worried about last night? Not if the disease had come back but how, if it had, it would affect you.' Tom took his hand away. 'So I made a decision. Meeting you was one of the best things in my life—perhaps the best thing. It made me change my mind about how

I was going to live—but now I'm going to have to change back. Nikki, we—'

'Just a minute.' She raised her voice. 'Just stop there! For a minute just don't say anything!' Then she stopped, took out a handkerchief, wiped her face, blew her nose. This just would not do. She was a nurse and she was almost shouting at a patient in hospital—who also was the man she loved. She had to sympathise with his cares and his worries, even if she didn't agree with them.

She wanted to be calm but she knew her voice was still unsteady. 'Whatever it is, I can stand it,' she said at last. 'So long as I'm with you, Tom. You must let me make my own decisions.'

He grinned at her. 'Hey, Nurse,' he said, 'you're not supposed to shout at ill patients. You're supposed to be tender and calm and thoughtful and smooth my fevered brow.'

It was a joke, she knew, but it made her feel worse. How could he joke in this situation? It just meant that he wasn't going to be swayed by argument.

'You're going to tell me again that you're not going to put me through the agony of watching you suffer. Or, even worse, wonder if you're going to suffer. Right?'

'Something like that,' he admitted.

'Well, too bad! That agony's mine if I choose to take it. My life, my decision.' Wildly, she went on, 'I know you haven't asked me, but if after a while we thought that that's what we wanted, then I'd want us to spend the rest of our lives together. And if your life is to be short then a year's happiness is worth any price. Right?'

He lay there, saying nothing. 'I'm a poor nurse,

aren't I?' she mumbled after a moment. 'I shouldn't get at a patient like this.'

'Oh, yes, you should. It's one of the things that I love about you. You say exactly what you mean.'

There didn't seem to be much more to say for the moment. Both were silent. She reached out to take his hand, but he moved it away.

'I learned something, watching my mother die,' he said, 'and that was that it hurts more if you put off accepting the inevitable.' He scowled, as if at some unwelcome memory. 'I'll tell you something I've never admitted to anyone, Nikki. In fact, I didn't admit it to myself for many years. But…I was glad when my mother finally died. Not only because I wanted her to be out of pain, though I certainly did that. No, it was because I'd just got tired of waiting. She was going to die, we all knew that. So why didn't she die quickly?'

'You were young then, just a child. You couldn't be expected to—'

'I can be as stubborn as you. You showed me something I thought I'd never have—the prospect of a happiness I could only imagine. I don't want to risk repaying you by having you watch me die, have the love between us slowly lapse into irritation. I'll be back at work by the end of the week. Now, seeing you here only makes me feel worse. I want you to go straight back home. As soon as I get back to Hambleton I'll tell Joe that I want to leave as soon as it's convenient. We have to part, Nikki.'

'No!' she wailed. 'We need time. Perhaps you—'

'Nikki, I've never asked you anything much. I'm asking you this to make it easier for me. Accept what

I'm saying. What we had has no future. So we cut it out now.'

'Cut it out? Like surgery?'

'Just like surgery. Will you do this for me, Nikki?'

'I think I hate you now! How can you do this to me?'

The door opened and the ward sister glanced in. Nikki knew that she could detect the atmosphere in the room. The sister looked at her sympathetically but her voice was firm.

'I'm sorry,' she said, 'but the patient is tired. Perhaps you ought to go.'

Nikki looked down at Tom, half expecting him to object, to say that she should stay. But he said nothing. And he *did* look tired. Nikki accepted that the sister was right.

She leaned over, kissed Tom's cheek. He didn't respond. Then she followed the sister out of the room.

'You're suffering, too, aren't you?' the sister said. 'I can tell. Would you like a drink?'

'I'll be all right,' said Nikki, 'but thank you so much.'

Nikki drove straight back home. She knew that Tom was quite capable of refusing to see her if she arrived at his bedside next morning. After a restless night she went to the surgery. She knew that Joe always arrived an hour before he needed to see his first patient. She could talk to him.

Joe made her a coffee and took her into his consulting room. They wouldn't be disturbed there. 'We're old friends, Nikki,' he said. 'I can guess what you're going through. I did try to warn you. Perhaps

I should have been more exact. I never expected
things to get this bad.'

'It was my own fault. I'm a big girl now, I make
my own mistakes. And Tom couldn't have been
fairer. I think he's suffering emotionally as much as
I am.'

'Quite possibly. He could have been a fine GP, he
has that feeling for people that is so important.
Still…he phoned me this morning and explained a
couple of things. It appears that this was just a false
alarm, though they're keeping him in a while to carry
out more tests.'

'He told me that,' she said flatly.

Joe looked uncomfortable. 'He also said that he
doesn't want to see you again at the hospital. You're
not to go down there and visit. He says he knows
about your good wishes, but that visiting him would
be…unproductive.'

Unproductive! That was a fine word. She said, 'It
doesn't really surprise me. He knows what he wants
and he goes for it.'

'My own opinion, for what it's worth,' Joe said
after a while, 'is to do as he says. It's best to leave
him alone for a while. He needs time to think, to get
over this scare. You can only distress him.'

'Did he…did he say anything about coming back
here?' Nikki asked hesitantly.

'He told me he thought it best if he resigned, that
his presence wasn't good for the well-being of the
surgery. Of course he would stay as long as was necessary until I could find another locum. I told him
that I didn't want to lose him, but that if he wanted
to go I wouldn't stand in his way.'

'I see,' she said. 'You will let me know how his case is getting on?'

'Of course,' said Joe.

Perhaps she could find solace in work. Later on that morning Nikki called round at the Ghyllhead nursing home and talked to George Dunmore. He was very happy there. Twice a day he talked to Mary on the telephone and they were planning a different future.

'We've been in that farmhouse too long, Nikki. It's time it went to someone younger, someone who could make a go of it. I've been talking to Marion Watts at Social Services. She says that she can arrange for us to move into one of those almshouses at the bottom of the village. It's called sheltered accommodation. You're independent but there's a warden there if you need one.'

'That'll be great, George! And there's a fantastic view out the back.'

'Yes, there's a view all right. I don't think I could be happy if there wasn't a fell for me to look at.'

While she was at the nursing home she called in to see Lucie Thrale. Lucie, a tremendously fit eighty-year-old, had just had minor surgery on her face. A plastic surgeon had cut out a rodent ulcer, a slow-growing skin cancer, from near her nose. Nikki checked the dressing and all was well.

'You'll have to use more sunblock in future, Lucie. You got that ulcer because of too much sun-bathing.'

'I like a good tan, it goes very well with my silver hair. I'm just trying a new hairstyle. What do you think, Nikki?'

'It's really nice. I like the way it's shaped round your ears.'

Lucie felt that just because she was getting on a bit, there was no need to let standards slip. She never appeared at breakfast without her hair brushed, her eyes made up and her lipstick carefully applied. Since she'd had her operation she had never appeared in public without a large pair of sunglasses. 'Takes people's eyes off that nasty dressing,' she told Nikki.

If Lucie and George can be as resilient as that, why can't I be? Nikki wondered as she drove away. I've got so much more to look forward to. I'm young, fit, healthy, have a good job, am reasonably good-looking. But it did little good. All she could feel was bleakness at the prospect of life without Tom.

She tried to put in a full, hard day, visiting people who didn't need visits, taking more pains than were really necessary. Then she got back late to her car-avan and cleaned it from end to end. Not that it took too long. But she couldn't help glancing at the back of the White House, now almost hidden by trees. There was no light in it. Nothing for her there.

The following Monday Tom came back. Nikki had been wondering how she would greet him. Should she go over to the White House if she saw a light in the back kitchen? Or should she invite him to the caravan for a meal? Perhaps they could talk and... But she knew it was impossible.

Somehow she had shut off all feelings. She did her work, smiled at her patients then retreated to her car-avan. She wanted to see no friends, have no social life. She didn't want to confide in anyone. She just existed in a grey world with no prospect of any improvement.

And she was appalled at her reaction when she saw Tom for the first time. She was totally unprepared. She was picking up supplies from the surgery when he came into the storeroom. And there was an instant searing flame. This was the man she loved!

He looked thinner—if that was possible—and certainly paler. But he was the old Tom and all her feelings for him stormed through her.

She felt shy, tongue-tied, and took refuge in formality. 'Good to see you, Tom. How are you?'

That wasn't what she'd wanted to say! Didn't he know what she was feeling?

But he was also determined to be formal, perhaps it was easier for him.

'I'm much better, thanks. It was a false alarm, as we'd thought, so now I'm looking forward to working my last couple of weeks here.'

'Last couple of weeks?' What did he mean?

'Joe thinks the practice can manage without me after that—he's come to some arrangement with a practice in the next village. There's various things I have to do and then I'll be out of your life for good.' He paused and then said, 'I'll try to keep out of your way. We'll see each other a few more times but only professionally.'

'Professionally! Is that it, then? What about what we mean to each other? You can't deny it, you love me just as much as I love you!'

'It'll fade, Nikki, it'll have to. That's why I'm leaving, so you can get on with your life.'

'How can you bear to leave me?'

He had turned to the door, was walking away. As she spoke he stopped and she saw his back go rigid.

He turned back. 'How can I bear it? I can't bear it!'

His lips came down on hers in a kiss that left her senses reeling. It was a kiss like the one on top of Cragend Hill, a kiss of desperation as much as passion.

'Don't you ever think that it's not as hard for me as it is for you!'

Then he was gone.

CHAPTER NINE

PERHAPS he or Joe arranged it that way, but for the next few days she didn't see Tom once. At night, just before Nikki went to bed, she'd look out of her window, and perhaps there'd be a light on in the White House. But she never went over to him. And even though they were neighbours, he never came over to call on her.

She carried on with her work, it was the one thing that kept her sane. She was miserable but she had to work. And then on Friday the weather changed and that made things worse. They'd had an incredibly long period of fine weather, now it looked as if it would break.

It made her feel worse. The very air felt sticky, there was no breeze and the sky turned an evil yellow colour. No matter what she wore, what cosmetics she used, after ten minutes she could feel the sweat collecting under her arms, running down between her breasts.

Everyone was irritable. Patients snapped at her. The staff at the surgery had the sense not to get angry but they kept out of each other's way. For the first time ever Nikki felt that she hated her job. Half-seriously, she started to wonder about leaving the moors, about starting a completely new life somewhere. She had heard there were good jobs to be had in America, Arizona had been mentioned. Or perhaps she should give city life a chance and move…not to London but perhaps somewhere like Birmingham.

But she knew she wouldn't move. For a start, it would take too much effort. The weather was nothing really. She was just miserable.

She was on her morning rounds out on the moors and suddenly the sky became darker. The sticky air grew cooler, for the first time in days Nikki wound up her window. There was even a chilly breeze. She knew what was going to happen and switched on her lights.

A couple of raindrops smacked onto her windscreen. There was a distant hiss and, with a noise like paper tearing, the rain deluged down. Headlights on, she drove slowly for a while then pulled off into a layby. Visibility was so bad it was unsafe to drive.

After a while the rain settled into a steady beating on her car and she decided to drive home. There were no calls that were too urgent and she felt that she was just a hazard on the road. She guessed that there'd be more than a few accidents before the day was done—Joe's surgery would be busy.

She went back to her caravan. It was noisy, with the drumming of rain on her roof. She made herself a snack lunch and then left half of it. The lights came on in the kitchen of the White House. Should she go over there and attempt to reason with Tom? No point. He'd said all that was necessary. Besides, she was too dispirited to do anything needing so much emotional energy.

It rained like this about once every five years. Certainly the crops needed it, but it was going to cause chaos in the little town. She didn't care. She didn't care much about anything.

It got dark early and she saw the lights go out in the kitchen of the White House. It didn't concern her. She sat there in the dark, not wanting to eat, find company or do anything. What was the point?

At eleven o'clock the phone rang. Who could it be at this hour of night? For a moment she was tempted to ignore it. The last thing she needed was a friendly chat with someone. But it might be something serious. She picked up the phone. It *was* serious.

'Nikki?' It was Tom's voice! She wouldn't have thought her spirits could change so quickly. For a moment she was speechless, wondering what he wanted. Perhaps he'd changed his mind, perhaps he—

'Nikki, are you there?'

The voice sounded driven, urgent, and she began to suspect that it wasn't her he really wanted, that this was business. Not work at this hour of night! Not with Tom! 'Yes, what is it, Tom?'

'Nikki, this isn't the way I wanted to talk to you, but this is a real emergency. There's been an accident in Greenpot Cavern.'

'An accident,' she repeated dully.

'Yes, I'm afraid so. I'm there now. One of the outlying caverns flooded because of this sudden rainfall and four potholers had to get out quickly. They weren't very experienced, they had to take a harder route out and they all fell. Now one is trapped and three have been injured. The rescue team has managed to get three of them into a cavern that's more or less safe, but they'd like a doctor to see them before they're carried out. I've volunteered and I'll be going down in about fifteen minutes. Nikki, I need a nurse to come with me. I've phoned round but you're the only one available. This rainstorm has caused chaos. Can you get here in a quarter of an hour?'

Nikki's mouth was dry—did he know what he was asking her? For the moment all feelings for him disappeared, weren't important. This was nothing to do with him. What was important was the prospect of going underground. She was terrified at the very thought. Already her palms were damp and there was a light beading of sweat on her forehead. To go underground—into those dark wet caverns. People got caught in them, trapped in them, sometimes they died down there. She sobbed. She just couldn't do it.

'Can you hear me, Nikki? Can you get here in a quarter of an hour?'

'Tom, I can't do it, I just can't.'

His voice was a little impatient. 'It won't be very nice, I know, but they're a good team here. They assure me there's no risk. It'll mean crawling through mud and so on but it'll be quite safe. They've got wetsuits and all the specialised kit to lend you.'

'You don't understand! It's not that I just don't want to—I can't! I'm claustrophobic. I told you once before. I want to help but, Tom, I just couldn't!'

His voice softened. 'Of course, I remember now, you did tell me. Don't worry, sweetheart, I'm sure I can manage.'

It was calling her 'sweetheart' that did it. That and the fact that she was a nurse. She was needed! She knew that her fear was unreasonable, that unreasonable fears could be conquered. It was time that she conquered this fear. And Tom would be there. He would give her strength. 'Tom, I'll be there in fifteen minutes,' she said, and rang off before she could change her mind.

Why had she said it? She closed her eyes, tried to imagine what it would be like and smiled bleakly. She could do it! Women much younger—and much older—than her did it for fun, so she could do it. And Tom would be there.

She grabbed her anorak and hat and ran out to the car. Greenpot Cavern wasn't too far away and she knew the road. It was just as well. In several places there were streams running over the road and she was glad of her four-wheel-drive. Concentrating on driving was good for her, it took her mind off the horrors ahead. She would just get there. Then perhaps they'd decide they didn't really need her. Not much of a chance, she thought bitterly. Tom would only have phoned her if she was necessary. He didn't want to see her, even to work with.

She turned off into the field that held the entrance to Greenpot Cavern, bumping slowly across the grass. Ahead of her she saw lights, a cluster of vehicles, the hut that cavers used as headquarters.

When she'd parked, a policeman came over to ask who she was. She told him she was a nurse and was going to go down the cavern. He held her door for her, took her arm to make sure she didn't slip. She didn't like the unnecessary care. What would she have to do to earn it?

Inside the hut it was like a scene from a science fiction film. Burly men stood round in shiny black wetsuits, lights fixed to their heads. Others were organising great lengths of rope, metal ladders, other kit she didn't recognise. But she did recognise the stretchers. They were designed so that patients could be strapped inside them and then hoisted or lowered down cliff faces. Even if the patient was turned upside down he couldn't slide out or come to any harm. Well, that was the theory.

And there was Tom, in a wetsuit like the others, carefully checking a box of medical supplies. He looked up at her and his eyes were compassionate. 'You don't have to do this, Nikki,' he said. 'I'm sure I'll manage without you.'

That angered her, which was a surprise. She hadn't thought she had enough emotion left after fear to be angry.

'I can do it,' she said. 'I'm a nurse and I can do it if I'm needed.'

He reached over and squeezed her shoulder. 'I know you can. I knew I could rely on you.'

Rely on her for what? Well, that was another story. She said, 'Anyway, are *you* up to it? You've just had a stay in hospital, you don't look too brilliant to me.'

He frowned. 'I know that—one reason why I so much wanted you here. But I've got to be up to it. If you're a nurse then I'm a doctor and it sounds like these men need more than simple first aid.' He looked over her shoulder. 'Luke, have you got a wetsuit Nikki's size?'

A man looked at her and spoke, his cultured voice seeming at odds with the filthy wetsuit he was wearing. 'Miss Gale, I'm Luke Meadows in charge of cave rescue here. We're very grateful to have you with us. Do you know how to put this on?' He offered her a wetsuit.

'I've been waterskiing in one,' she muttered. 'I guess I'll cope.'

She was shown into a back room to change, and

fumbled her way out of her clothes and into the sticky hot garment. This was going to be torture. Then she went outside to be fitted with a light on her head and a belt holding the battery. 'What do I carry?' she asked.

Luke answered. 'We've got experienced men as porters. All you have to do is get yourself down. Simon here will be your minder and lead you down into the cave.'

Simon, a man in his forties, with a big black moustache, smiled at her. 'It'll be no trouble,' he said. 'Shall we go?'

The party was setting off.

She walked out of the hut, stood for a moment in the rain. Never had it seemed so welcoming. Then she made for the open door that led into the blackness of Greenpot Cavern.

At first it wasn't too bad. They walked in single file along a passage with the occasional fixed light. Like the others, she turned on her head light and concentrated on looking at the little circle of light as it lit the floor in front of her.

Simon seemed to sense what she was going through. He kept up a flow of chatter to take her mind off things. He was a bank manager, he could get her a mortgage, did she want any advice about money? He would give it to her happily. And she didn't think of what was to come.

But then they came to the end of the passage and started the proper caving. They had to slide down a steep passage, perhaps four feet in width. It was dark—and as Nikki saw the blackness ahead of her, and felt the monotonous dropping of water onto her, she felt the terror rising.

'Just give me a minute,' she muttered to Simon.

She could see Tom ahead, the line of his neck and shoulder was unmistakable. Some mysterious power must have told him that she was looking at him. He turned and waved. It wasn't much, but she guessed it was all she was going to get. This suffering on top of what else he had put her through. She decided that Tom owed her now. Not that she could ever claim from him.

Tom and his minder disappeared into that appalling hole. She watched and shuddered, then turned to Simon.

'Let's do it,' she said.

Once she'd started it wasn't too hard. She'd done quite a bit of scrambling on the Moors—indeed, had been a rock-climber for a while. She found she was quite at home negotiating the piles of stones, the tiny rockfaces. After a while Simon left her alone, deciding she could manage. Quickly they caught up with Tom and his minder and had to wait. She realised that Tom wasn't quite as practised as she was and felt a tiny touch superior—but not much. Having to stop reminded her of all the rock above her, and she shivered with terror.

'Will—will you be able to get those stretchers up here?' she asked Simon.

'We've practised often enough. Yes, we'll be able to do it.'

Then the passage she was in got narrower and narrower, and she had to get down on her hands and knees. She didn't know if she'd be able to crawl through it, but somehow she did it. Then she crawled out into a much larger chamber and it was time to be professional.

There were three men lying on the floor with a group of others clustered anxiously round them. They moved back readily as Tom and Nikki arrived, happy to give way to the experts.

Tom immediately bent over the one man who was unconscious—good triage practice. Nikki knelt by the other two, smiled and said, 'Hello, I'm Nikki Gale—I'm a nurse. This is Tom Murray—he's a doctor. You have made a mess of yourselves, haven't you? Let's see if we can make you more comfortable.' She got weak smiles back.

The unconscious man was worst hurt. He had fallen and severed an artery in his arm and his friends had put on a tourniquet. Very properly they had then loosened it from time to time to ensure that gangrene didn't set in, but this meant that he had lost a lot of blood. With Nikki's help Tom roughly closed the cut, but they had to do something about the lost blood. From the medical kit Tom took a giving set, filled it with plasma and set the needle into a vein. 'It'll keep him going till he gets to hospital,' he whispered to Nikki.

The second man was complaining of a violent headache. Tom fitted him with a neck brace and felt round the skull for signs of a fracture. Not that there was much he could do if he found one. There were probably a couple of ribs broken, too. Nikki strapped them up.

They worked well as a team for perhaps half an hour. She knew that Tom could have managed without her. She also knew that she was being a great help to him. She saved him time, she saved the three injured men pain. He needed a nurse. The tiny feeling of professional pride gave her strength.

Finally they supervised as the three men were carefully loaded into their stretchers, tightly strapped in. Then a team set off to carry each to the surface. As Simon had told her, they were trained for this and had practised often. Her job and Tom's were now finished. There were already ambulances waiting for them. Luke was in constant contact with the surface.

She didn't want to think about anything, she wanted to concentrate on her job. That way she didn't need to worry about the great weight of rock that sometimes seemed to be pressing onto her, stopping her even breathing.

She kept her head bowed and was aware that Luke had appeared from somewhere and was muttering to Tom. Tom said, 'I'll be back in ten minutes, Nikki. You all right here?'

'Never better.' She had meant to sound confident—but by the sharp way he looked at her she knew he'd recognised her desperate tone.

Tom left anyway, and she huddled on a rock, her head down. Simon came and sat next to her but said nothing. She was still glad of his presence.

Then Tom came back and as she flashed her light up to his face she saw the strained expression there. 'Where's the fourth man?' she asked, a horror too deep to be contemplated welling up inside her. 'Didn't you say he was…he was trapped?'

Trapped? Down here? Her head swam just to contemplate it.

'Yes, there's a man here and he's trapped. We haven't got him out yet, though we're working on it.'

Perhaps it was her heightened awareness, perhaps there was something in his voice, but Nikki's terror returned tenfold. 'What...what are you going to do? What's the problem?'

She didn't really want to know what the problem was. She wanted to get out of this dreadful place, away from the darkness, the constant dripping of water, the sense of pressure from all those millions of tons of rock.

'He's in the next cavern to this. A crack runs across the floor—this group didn't know about it. The fourth man slipped and fell down the crack. A lot of loose rocks fell with him and on top of him. He's down about fifteen feet, we can just see a bit of his head. He's unconscious, could be dead. Certainly he'll die soon if we don't get him out. We need to get someone down to get a rope round his chest. Then we can pull him up. Everyone here has tried to get down, even me. We're all too big.'

A thought was hammering at her brain, a suspicion that she didn't even want to consider. But Tom said it for her. 'The only person here who is slim enough to get down the crack is you.'

She had to ask. 'There's no one else could do it?'

'They've already sent for an experienced caver. She's a young girl, only fourteen, but she'd do this like a shot. The trouble is, she's on holiday somewhere. We can't find her or her family, but the police are trying to trace her.' He smiled. 'You've done well to do this much, Nikki. We'll get someone to take you to the surface.'

The words seemed to stick in her throat, as if they didn't want to be said, but she said them anyway. 'Not yet. At least let me have a look at this crack.'

Simon and Tom led her, scrambling through another low tunnel to a smaller chamber. Lights had been rigged over the crack. Around it were men in wetsuits, peering downwards. To one side there was a nearly naked man being helped back into his wet-suit. Nikki saw the bloody scratches on his chest, where he'd obviously tried to force himself down-wards. Could she suffer the same?

The group fell silent as she approached. She guessed they knew that she was the man's last chance—and the weight of that knowledge was heavy on her. She couldn't do this! Any nursing job, yes, no matter how dangerous, but to bury herself like this? Then, from somewhere, came a touch of pride. She'd been terrified but she'd got this far. She could conquer her fear. No way would she give up now. She would follow this job through to its bitter end.

She leaned over and peered downwards, aware of Tom's hand on her arm. The walls of the crack were black and shiny with water. She could just see a bit of the man—the redness of his helmet, a bit of his wetsuit. Opposite her, a man shouted, 'Can you hear us, Barry?'

There was no answer from below. The man looked up and said, 'We heard him moaning earlier on. We dropped him a telephone—but it did no good.'

Think of it as the narrow space between a cup-board and a wall, she told herself. You're squeezing in there to get a paper. You know you're slimmer than anyone here—you can do things they can't. Out of nowhere came the memory of her first meeting with Tom. He had called her thin and she had told him she preferred to be called slim. Why think of that now? To stop you thinking of what you've got to do, came the answer. And to get you to forget that this isn't a cupboard and a wall. If you're in trouble, a cupboard can be moved.

'What needs to be done?' she asked.

It was Luke, in charge of the rescue, who answered. 'If we could get this harness on him and a rope to him, we could pull him up,' he said. 'The walls are smooth and he'd slide up easily.' He showed her the harness, a set of straps. She had used one before when she'd been rock-climbing.

'Do...do you think I could do it?' she asked.

'More easily than any of us,' Luke answered, 'and you'd be quite safe. You'd have a separate rope round you.'

Safe? Was anyone safe down here? 'You would...you would keep the rope tight?' she asked.

Luke looked at her and she could see the fatigue in his face. 'I can guess what you're going through,' he said. 'We don't even want you to try if you're going to panic. And we all panic at times. You have to hang onto yourself.'

Tom was by her side. 'You don't have to do this, Nikki,' he said. 'You've done more than enough already. Perhaps it would be better if we waited until the expert arrives and—'

'That man will be dead soon, won't he?' she asked.

Tom's silence answered her question.

'I'll do it while I dare,' she said. 'Like now. But how do I bend over to put the harness on him?'

Then came the final horror. 'We lower you down head first,' said Luke.

There was a harness round her and a thick rope led upwards between her legs to the men above. In her hands was another rope and harness. She was to brush the debris away from Barry and then fix the harness round his chest. Attached to her helmet was a tiny telephone set so she would be in touch with Luke all the time. Time to do it.

She knelt on the edge of the crack, slid slowly forward. One last horrified thought—this was like diving into a grave. Then she was inching downwards. Somehow she managed to close off her terror, to concentrate only on what had to be done.

They lowered her slowly. She did as Tom had told her, breathed in and out gently, tried to hold her heartbeat steady, never ever made any sudden movements. Her body should relax! Hard to do when rock was pressing in on her at every side. If she breathed in really deeply she could jam herself in the crack. But she pulled herself ever downwards.

The beam of her helmet shone ahead. Here the crack bent a little, which had made it hard to see Barry. Somehow she scraped round. And then she reached him.

'I'm there,' she reported to Luke. 'Six more inches and then hold me. I'll brush the bits of stone off him.'

Barry was covered in clay and bits of damp rock. Nikki brushed them aside, making sure they fell right down the crack. 'Barry, can you hear me?' There was no reply. Then she felt down for the pulse in his neck. It was there, but very weak. Barry had to have medical attention quickly.

Next she tried to put the harness on, pushing it down between the wall of the crack and his back— and it wasn't possible! She brushed more of the bits of rock away and the full horror of what had happened became clear. Was there to be no end to her torment? As he'd fallen Barry's left arm had twisted behind his back. It was stuck there. There was no way she could free it—and without freeing it Barry couldn't be pulled upwards. 'He's jammed tight! He'll never get free!' she panted into the mouthpiece. 'I don't know what to do!'

Tom answered—he must have been standing next to Luke. 'First thing, just hang there,' he said. 'Don't do anything for a minute, just close your eyes and see if you can relax. Take a couple of breaths. You're doing fine. This is a problem and problems have solutions. Just try and take it easy for a minute.'

'You try taking it easy when you're helpless, hanging upside down and terrified,' she retorted.

'That's a good point. Now, describe exactly where Barry's arm is, why he can't be pulled up.'

She did so. He asked for further details, wanting to know to the nearest couple of inches where Barry's arm was trapped. Having to concentrate on answering took her mind off things and she felt less afraid.

'Can you put your hand on a large stone, about the size of a fist?'

That was an odd question. She scrabbled round, found one. 'There's one here. Why?'

The pause before he replied should have warned her of the further horror to come. 'I've worked out what you have to do for Barry. Take the rock and smash it in the middle of his clavicle. Break the bone.'

'*What?*'

'Then his shoulder will collapse and you'll be able to free his arm.'

'You want me to hang upside down, take a rock

and smash a man's shoulder bone? Tom, that's the
most bizarre thing I've—'

'Nikki! You're losing it. Get a grip! Break that
clavicle. You can do it for me…and I love you.'

I love you. She wondered if there had ever been a
declaration like that one.

She assessed the weight of the rock in her hand.
Then she told herself that this wasn't a bone, it didn't
belong to a human being. It was a branch of a tree
and it was slowly killing Barry. Then she told herself
that there would be no practising. The bone would
break at the first blow.

And it did.

She felt sick at the sound, the feel of it. But then
she pushed at the arm—the shoulder collapsed and
distorted as Tom had said it would—and she was
able to get the harness on. She clipped on Barry's
rope. 'Pull me up slowly a couple of feet,' she called,
'then try and pull Barry up.'

It was weird, being pulled backwards. She pointed
her toes, tried to kick off from the sides of the crack.
Then she stopped and the men above, very cau-
tiously, started to pull on Barry's rope. It tightened.
She felt it hard against her shoulder, her thigh.
'Gently,' she cried, 'gently… He's moving!'

The body below her edged slowly upwards and
she reached down and steadied the lolling head.
'Now pull me up another foot and then Barry another
foot!'

It was working! Barry slid round the bend in the
crack, came up towards her. She felt again for the
pulse in the neck. Still there—he was still alive.

'Now another foot!' It wasn't exactly easy, but it
was easier. And there was the distant feeling of hope

and even triumph. The job was being done, it was a success. And soon she would be out.

A foot upwards and then another foot upwards and then another. Nikki didn't know where she was—but suddenly there were hands grasping her feet, then her legs, and she was hauled out, turned the right way up. She swayed, someone put his arms round her, supported her and lowered her to the ground.

'Nikki! Are you all right?' Tom was leaning over her.

'I'll live. Look after Barry, he's the one who needs you.'

Tom bent over and hugged her. 'We're still doctor and nurse. But in an hour or so we can be human beings as well. Now, I need to check over Barry before we move him. And you're going straight to the surface. No arguments.'

'But don't you need a—?'

'I've just asked you to do more than I've ever asked another human being to do before. And it was harder because I am…close to you. Now, go while you can still walk.'

'How is Barry?'

'He's alive, and thanks to you he has a fighting chance of staying that way. Go!'

It wasn't just Simon who helped her to the surface, another man came with him. And she needed them both. Much of the time they half carried her. But then they were walking along the lamplit corridor, and finally they were out in the open air. It was still raining. She thought that she'd never before felt anything so wonderful.

There were more people gathered in the hut now. A paramedic took her into the back room, helped her out of the wetsuit and checked her over. She was given the traditional mug of hot sweet tea and she thought she'd never enjoyed a drink so much. When she staggered out of the back room the two men were waiting for her, both having changed out of their wetsuits. 'I'll drive you straight home,' said Simon, 'and Ralph here will follow me in your car.'

'All right,' said Nikki. She was beyond making any further decisions, everything had to be done for her. She was escorted to a car, eased in and her seat belt fastened for her. Simon drove. 'You can talk if you want to,' he said in a kind voice, 'but I suspect you want just to be left alone.'

'If you don't mind. I'm sorry, I don't want to be rude but...'

'That's OK. I understand. Just one thing. Barry's a friend of mine and you saved his life. So, thank you.'

'I'm a nurse. We do what we can,' she said simply.

Once at the caravan Simon and Ralph saw her inside, made sure there was nothing that she needed and asked if they should phone anyone. She said, no, she was tired but she would be fine. When they had gone she stripped off her clothes and showered—for the longest she had ever showered in her life. She could detect something on her body—the smell of clay and darkness—and she never wanted to smell it again.

Then she towelled herself dry, put on her bathrobe and made herself another drink. And as she sat on her couch the hard defences she had hidden behind for the past few hours slowly crumbled away. She remembered how her terror had mounted, from going down the cavern to going down the crack to breaking Barry's arm. How had she done it? Tasks accomplished were supposed to seem easier afterwards. This one didn't. She shuddered. How had she done it?

Someone knocked at her door. She glanced at her clock—it was two in the morning, not a usual time for visitors. Never mind, it had been an unusual day. She wasn't even surprised.

It was Tom, as bedraggled as she had been. 'Barry's going to survive,' he said. 'We thought we'd lost him a couple of times but he's going to survive. He's got a wife and a couple of kids. Think what you did for them, Nikki.'

Unbelievably, she felt angry. 'He had no business going down there when he had a family,' she shouted. 'The man must be mad. What do you want anyway?'

'I saw your light was on. I'm exhausted and I know you are. I wanted to see you and I want to borrow your shower and have a drink with you. I just want to be next to you.'

'I'll put the kettle on,' she said. 'Will you go back to the White House later?'

'No. I need to be in bed with you.'

CHAPTER TEN

THEY didn't make love, they were far too tired. But it was so good to go to sleep with her head on Tom's arm, with the warmth of his breath on her face. Next morning Nikki slept on, only waking when he brought a tray of tea and toast to her bedside.

'Eat,' he ordered when she tried to protest. 'You need to get your strength up, so eat. We'll talk later.'

'But I've got a couple of calls to make. I know it's Saturday but—'

'I phoned Joe last night. I was supposed to be covering the weekend but neither of us is working today. That was his decision not mine. He said we'd done enough.'

'But, Tom, there are things we—'

'Eat first. Things will wait.'

She remembered Mrs Ravensby telling her about things, and felt rather warm. But she ate as he'd told her and afterwards felt definitely stronger. He put the tray on the floor and they sat there, looking at each other. Both of them had slept without clothes. She pulled the sheet up over her breasts and he leaned over and pulled it down again. 'A small pleasure, looking at you like this,' he said. 'No, it isn't, it's a large pleasure.'

She looked at him demurely. 'Are we going to—?'

'No, we're not. Well, not until we've had a talk. This is serious, Nikki.'

'I'm fed up with being serious. I'm the serious one. And it's hard when we're both naked.'

'You'll just have to put up with it.'

She knew that he was determined to say what he wanted to, but she sighed loudly and pushed the sheet even further down the bed.

'Later,' he said firmly, and stared at her dressing-table until she pulled the sheet up a little.

'You were terrified last night,' he said. 'I don't think I've ever seen such fear on anyone's face. But first you came into the cavern and then you volunteered to be lowered into that appalling crack. I can only guess at what you went through. But you did it, for a complete stranger. I think you're the strongest woman I know. I think you could stand anything.'

He paused, but she said nothing. Her heart was beating so violently she couldn't speak. What was he going to say?

'I think you could stand anything,' he repeated. 'So I'm going to be completely selfish. You know the situation I'm in. You know what could happen. And in spite of that...will you marry me? No one could love you more than I do. But I don't want an answer straight way, I'd like you to think about it for a while. Talk to people, there are others who—'

'Of course I'll marry you.' Nikki was incandescent with joy. 'No one could make me happier. And I don't want to ask other people. I know what I want. I think I've wanted to marry you since you fell on my roof. And love isn't between two bodies—it's between two people, two souls. Love can transcend pain and sometimes pain can even strengthen love. Yes, I'll marry you. So you can kiss me now.'

And after a while she murmured, 'I said kiss, but if you want to…'

They wanted to get married quickly. And things suddenly seemed to be working so well for them that it seemed as if the world was conspiring to make them happy. They went to see Penny Pink and commissioned her to make the ring they had both so much liked. The stone was of deepest emerald.

'There's something else,' Tom said. 'I'm not going back to London. Somehow this place has got to me. I feel I'm among friends, I like the pace of work here. If I can, I want to stay locally.'

'Tom! You're not just saying that to please me? Marriage is give and take. If you need to go back to London, I'll go with you.'

'I wouldn't dream of it,' he said.

And a week later they discovered that Anna Rix had written to Joe. She was very sorry but Floyd had been offered a fantastic job. She would be staying in America and wanted to give up her post as junior partner. Did Joe know anyone who might want to buy the White House? She would ideally like a quick sale.

'I've got nearly that much,' said Tom. 'I never spent my money when I was in hospital. Shall we buy it?'

'Tom! You know I've always loved the house, I can't think of anything nicer. But I want to decorate it all the way through, and I want new furniture!'

'Of course,' he said. 'And I'll put it in your name.'

'You'll do no such thing. You can put it in our joint names if you like, but that's all. What shall we do with the caravan?'

'Keep it,' he said. 'It's got so many happy memories. If we have a row, one of us can go and sit in it. The other will know where to come to make up.'

'We're not going to have rows. So, will you speak to Joe?'

'I already have. He pointed out that not only has he a house to sell, he has a position going as a junior partner. Of course, he can manage to start with a locum but...'

'Are you sure that this is what you want? You want to give up orthopaedics?'

'I've trained as a GP,' he reminded her. 'I can do the work and I like it.'

'Well, if you're sure...'

'I'm more than sure. I'm certain.'

It was a wonderful wedding. Nikki was the youngest child so by now her parents knew exactly what to do. And they were delighted. There was no shortage of brothers and sisters-in-law to offer advice.

Bridesmaids were a problem. She had to limit them to one from each family—but even so she finished up with six. A friend of her father lent them an open carriage and set of horses for the day so she drove up the main street of Hambleton to the parish church in style.

They had decided she would get married from the White House. They had their reception in a big marquee in the back garden and afterwards there was a disco at the Assembly Rooms.

Their honeymoon was short. They had so much to do, so little time. They went to a hotel high on the moors for three days and then came back to their new home.

It was again a lovely evening. For some reason they sat outside on the caravan patio and had a drink of cocoa together.

'This is the happiest day of my life,' Tom told her. 'I feel so lucky. I only hope that you will be…that is, that I…'

Nikki leaned over and kissed him. 'You're going to be fine,' she whispered lovingly. 'We have each other.'

EPILOGUE

IT TOOK time, of course, but two years later Nikki had the White House more or less as she wanted it. So many decisions to make! One good thing about living in a caravan had been that she'd been limited in her choices—there just hadn't been room for them. But here, in this spacious Georgian house, things were different.

She hadn't got all the furniture she wanted. She had started on the garden but it still needed a lot of work. And there was so much to do. Joe still called her out from time to time to do a little nursing.

'I'm back!' Tom came into the large kitchen where they seemed to spend so much of their time together.

He kissed her, then slipped his hand inside her loose shirt, put his hand on her swollen abdomen and smiled. 'I can feel him kicking,' he said.

'Or her kicking,' Nikki said reprovingly. 'I've got a feeling that it's going to be a girl.'

Nikki was more serene now, less likely to argue whenever there was a chance. She had her husband, her family, the house she had always coveted. Tom was working well with Joe, who was talking about going into semi-retirement and leaving Tom as the senior partner. How could she be happier?

Tom came to sit by her and kissed her again. 'Aren't you going to ask me how my trip went?' he asked.

He had been to the hospital in Leeds for his six-monthly check-up at the oncology clinic. The first couple of times she had insisted on going with him. It had been a waste of time, there had been nothing to report. Now he went on his own. He didn't need her support.

Calmly she said, 'I know how your trip went. Once again, nothing to report. Something just told me that that would be the case.'

'Very medical, very scientific. But I agree with you and you're right. One thing about Hodgkin's— if it doesn't get worse it gets better. There'll never be a complete certain cure...but I think I'll live as long as a normal man.'

'Of course you will.' She knew it was true.

He kissed her again. 'It doesn't seem fair, does it? After all, I've had a lifetime's happiness in the past two years anyway.'

'There's more happiness to come,' she said. 'Now there's you and me and soon there'll be another of us. We're happy because we're together, Tom. What I always wanted.'

'And what I always wanted, too.'

Modern Romance™
...seduction and
passion guaranteed

Tender Romance™
...love affairs that
last a lifetime

Sensual Romance™
...sassy, sexy and
seductive

Blaze
...sultry days and
steamy nights

Medical Romance™
...medical drama on
the pulse

Historical Romance™
...rich, vivid and
passionate

27 new titles every month.

*With all kinds of Romance for
every kind of mood...*

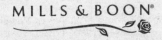

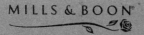

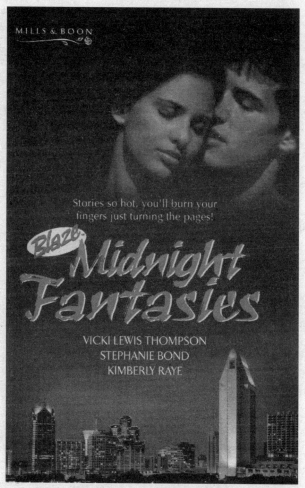

Don't miss *Book Two* of this BRAND-NEW 12 book collection 'Bachelor Auction'.

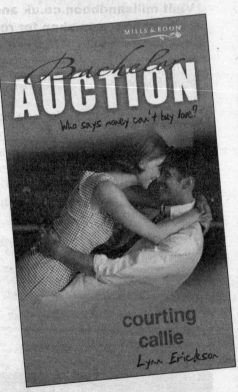

Who says
money
can't buy
love?

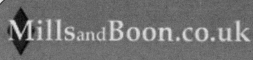

FREE
2 BOOKS
AND A SURPRISE GIFT!

We would like to take this opportunity to thank you for reading this Mills & Boon® book by offering you the chance to take TWO more specially selected titles from the Medical Romance™ series absolutely FREE! We're also making this offer to introduce you to the benefits of the Reader Service™ —

★ FREE home delivery
★ FREE monthly Newsletter
★ FREE gifts and competitions
★ Exclusive Reader Service discount
★ Books available before they're in the shops

Accepting these FREE books and gift places you under no obligation to buy; you may cancel at any time, even after receiving your free shipment. Simply complete your details below and return the entire page to the address below. *You don't even need a stamp!*

YES! Please send me 2 free Medical Romance books and a surprise gift. I understand that unless you hear from me, I will receive 4 superb new titles every month for just £2.55 each, postage and packing free. I am under no obligation to purchase any books and may cancel my subscription at any time. The free books and gift will be mine to keep in any case.

M2ZEC

Ms/Mrs/Miss/Mr ....Initials ....
BLOCK CAPITALS PLEASE

Surname ....

Address ....

....

....Postcode ....

Send this whole page to:
UK: FREEPOST CN81, Croydon, CR9 3WZ
EIRE: PO Box 4546, Kilcock, County Kildare (stamp required)

Offer valid in UK and Eire only and not available to current Reader Service subscribers to this series. We reserve the right to refuse an application and applicants must be aged 18 years or over. Only one application per household. Terms and prices subject to change without notice. Offer expires 31st December 2002. As a result of this application, you may receive offers from other carefully selected companies. If you would prefer not to share in this opportunity please write to The Data Manager at the address above.

Mills & Boon® is a registered trademark owned by Harlequin Mills & Boon Limited.
Medical Romance™ is being used as a trademark.